W9-CER-684

Ogres

of

Ohio

Here's what readers from around the country are saying about Johnathan Rand's *AMERICAN CHILLERS:*

"Your books are awesome! I have all the
AMERICAN CHILLERS and I keep them right
by my bed since I read them every week!"
-Tommy W, age 9, Michigan

"My dog chewed up TERRIBLE TRACTORS OF TEXAS,
and then he puked. Is that normal?"
-Carlos V., age 11, New Jersey

"Johnathan Rand's books are my favorite.
They're really creepy and scary!"
-Jeremy J., age 9, Illinois

"My whole class loves your books! I have two
of them and they are really, really cool."
-Katie R., age 12, California

"I never liked to read before, but now I read
all the time! The 'Chillers' series is great!"
-Lauren B., age 10, Ohio

"I love AMERICAN CHILLERS because they
are scary, but not too scary, because I don't want
to have nightmares."
-Adrian P., age 11, Maine

"I just finished Florida Fog Phantoms.
It is a freaky book! I really liked it."
-Daniel R., Michigan

"I read all of the books in the MICHIGAN CHILLERS series, and I just started the AMERICAN CHILLERS series. I really love these books!"
-*Andrew K., age 13 Montana*

"I have six CHILLERS books, and I have read them all three times! I hope I get more for my birthday. My sister loves them, too."
-*Jaquann D., age 10, Illinois*

"I just read KREEPY KLOWNS OF KALAMAZOO and it really freaked me out a lot. It was really cool!"
-*Devin W., age 8, Texas*

"THE MICHIGAN MEGA-MONSTERS was great! I hope you write lots more books!"
-*Megan P., age 12, Kentucky*

"All of my friends love your books! Will you write a book and put my name in it?"
-*Michael L., age 10, Ohio*

"These books are the best in the world!"
-*Garrett M., age 9, Colorado*

"We read your books every night. They are really scary and some of them are funny, too."
-*Michael & Kristen K., Michigan*

"I read THE MICHIGAN MEGA-MONSTERS in two days, and it was cool! When are you going to write one about Wisconsin?"
-*John G., age 12, Wisconsin*

"Johnathan Rand is my favorite author!"
-Kelly S., age 8, Michigan

"AMERICAN CHILLERS are great. I got one
for Christmas, and I loved it. Now, my sister
is reading it. When she's done, I'm going to
read it again."
-Joel F., age 13, New York

"I like the CHILLERS books because they are
fun to read. They are scary, too."
-Hannah K., age 11, Minnesota

"I read the MEGA-MONSTERS book and I
really liked it. Mr. Rand is a great writer."
-Ryan M., age 12, Arizona

"I LOVE AMERICAN CHILLERS!"
-Zachary R., age 8, Indiana

"I read your book to my little sister and
she got freaked out. I did, too!"
-Jason J., age 12, Ohio

"These books are my favorite! I love reading them!"
-Sarah N., age 10, New Jersey

"Your books are great. Please write more so I can read them.
-Dylan H., age 7, Tennessee

Other books by Johnathan Rand:

Michigan Chillers:

#1: Mayhem on Mackinac Island
#2: Terror Stalks Traverse City
#3: Poltergeists of Petoskey
#4: Aliens Attack Alpena
#5: Gargoyles of Gaylord
#6: Strange Spirits of St. Ignace
#7: Kreepy Klowns of Kalamazoo
#8: Dinosaurs Destroy Detroit
#9: Sinister Spiders of Saginaw
#10: Mackinaw City Mummies
#11: Great Lakes Ghost Ship
#12: AuSable Alligators
#13: Gruesome Ghouls of Grand Rapids
#14: Bionic Bats of Bay City

American Chillers:

#1: The Michigan Mega-Monsters
#2: Ogres of Ohio
#3: Florida Fog Phantoms
#4: New York Ninjas
#5: Terrible Tractors of Texas
#6: Invisible Iguanas of Illinois
#7: Wisconsin Werewolves
#8: Minnesota Mall Mannequins
#9: Iron Insects Invade Indiana
#10: Missouri Madhouse
#11: Poisonous Pythons Paralyze Pennsylvania
#12: Dangerous Dolls of Delaware
#13: Virtual Vampires of Vermont
#14: Creepy Condors of California
#15: Nebraska Nightcrawlers
#16: Alien Androids Assault Arizona
#17: South Carolina Sea Creatures
#18: Washington Wax Museum
#19: North Dakota Night Dragons
#20: Mutant Mammoths of Montana
#21: Terrifying Toys of Tennessee
#22: Nuclear Jellyfish of New Jersey
#23: Wicked Velociraptors of West Virginia
#24: Haunting in New Hampshire
#25: Mississippi Megalodon
#26: Oklahoma Outbreak
#27: Kentucky Komodo Dragons
#28: Curse of the Connecticut Coyotes
#29: Oregon Oceanauts
#30: Vicious Vacuums of Virginia

Freddie Fernortner, Fearless First Grader:

#1: The Fantastic Flying Bicycle
#2: The Super-Scary Night Thingy
#3: A Haunting We Will Go
#4: Freddie's Dog Walking Service
#5: The Big Box Fort
#6: Mr. Chewy's Big Adventure
#7: The Magical Wading Pool
#8: Chipper's Crazy Carnival
#9: Attack of the Dust Bunnies from Outer Space!
#10: The Pond Monster

Adventure Club series:

#1: Ghost in the Graveyard
#2: Ghost in the Grand
#3: The Haunted Schoolhouse

For Teens:

PANDEMIA: A novel of the bird flu and the end of the world
(written with Christopher Knight)

American Chillers Double Thrillers:

Vampire Nation &
Attack of the Monster Venus Melon

#2: Ogres of Ohio

Johnathan
Rand

An AudioCraft Publishing, Inc. book

Book storage and warehouses provided by Chillermania!©
Indian River, Michigan

Warehouse security provided by:
Lily Munster and Scooby-Boo

American Chillers #2: Ogres of Ohio
ISBN 13-digit: 978-1-893699-21-2

Librarians/Media Specialists:
PCIP/MARC records available at www.americanchillers.com

Cover illustration by Dwayne Harris
Cover layout and design by Sue Harring

Dickinson Press, Inc. Grand Rapids, MI USA Job #38311 01/26/2011

Ogres of Ohio

VISIT CHILLERMANIA!

WORLD HEADQUARTERS FOR BOOKS BY JOHNATHAN RAND!

Yooperland

Indian River

Alpena

Traverse City

MICHIGAN

CHILLERMANIA!

I-75 Exit 313 then south 1 mile!

Mt. Pleasant

Bay City

Grand Rapids

Lansing

Detroit

Kalamazoo

Visit the HOME for books by Johnathan Rand! Featuring books, hats, shirts, bookmarks and other cool stuff not available anywhere else in the world! Plus, watch the American Chillers website for news of special events and signings at *CHILLERMANIA!* with author Johnathan Rand! Located in northern lower Michigan, on I-75! Take exit 313 . . . then south 1 mile! For more info, call (231) 238-0338. And be afraid! Be veeeery afraaaaaaiiiid . . . .

"Well Danielle . . . what do you think?"

I almost didn't hear my dad ask the question. I was looking out the rain-streaked car window, staring up at the big, two-story house that was now our home.

"It's . . . it's huge," I replied, trying not to sound nervous.

But I was. I was really nervous. There was something about the house that was just . . .

Creepy.

11

"I think you'll like it here," Mom said. "The rooms are big, and there is a fireplace on both floors."

Through the rain, the dark house looked cold and uninviting.

"It looks kind of lonely," I said.

"That's because no one has lived here for a while," Dad said, turning the key and shutting off the car engine. "It needs someone like us to take care of it. In a few months from now, we'll have flowers all around. The lawn will be fresh and green, and it will look like a home. *Our* home."

Dad was wrong, of course. The house wouldn't be a home.

It would be a nightmare.

We just didn't know it yet.

Our move from Columbus, Ohio, to Sandusky, Ohio, happened pretty fast. Dad's company transferred him, and we needed to find a new home real quick. I knew I was going to miss my friends in Columbus, but I was pretty excited to move. Sandusky is a city in northern Ohio, and our home was only a few miles from

Lake Erie, one of the Great Lakes.

But best of all, Sandusky is home to a place called Cedar Point. It's a really cool amusement park with awesome roller coasters and rides. We went there once on a class field trip, and when my dad told me that we would be moving to Sandusky, I couldn't believe it! I'd be living only a few miles from Cedar Point!

Too cool.

Walking inside our new home for the first time was like walking into a cave. The windows had been boarded up, so everything was very dark. The floors were wood, and my wet sneakers squeaked as I walked down the hall.

"You can pick any room upstairs," Dad said. "Whichever one you want."

Awesome! My dorky brother was spending the week at Grandma and Grandpa's, so I got to pick the best room first!

I flipped a light switch in the hall and nothing happened. I tried it again.

Still nothing.

"Dad," I called out. "The lights don't work."

"The power is still shut off," he said. "The electric company will be out later today to turn it on. Hang on a sec."

His heavy footsteps echoed down the hall, and suddenly he appeared around a corner. He was carrying a flashlight.

"Take this," he said, handing me the light. "And be careful. All of the windows upstairs are boarded up, so it will be pretty dark."

"Don't stay up there long, Danielle," Mom called out from the kitchen. "We have a lot of unpacking to do."

Dad walked away, and his footsteps faded down the hall. I looked up at the dark, winding staircase, sweeping the flashlight beam over the steps. Outside, thunder cracked.

I took one step up, then another. One more.

Another jolt of thunder exploded outside as I took another step. Ten more steps and I would be on the second floor.

I kept going, unaware of the awful things that were going to happen to me.

For the record, I don't get spooked easily. My brother Derek, who is ten, is always trying to freak me out in some way or another, so I'm always on the lookout for his silly pranks.

But Derek was at Grandma and Grandpa's for the rest of the week, and I shouldn't have to worry about his goofy antics.

So when I saw the strip of light coming from beneath one of the bedroom doors, I knew that it wasn't my brother playing a joke on me.

How can that be? I thought, staring at the light coming from beneath the closed door. It glowed brightly, like there was a light on inside.

But that was impossible. Dad said there was no electricity in the house, and we wouldn't have any power until later in the day.

How could a light be on?

Just to be sure, I reached out and flipped a light switch on the wall.

Nothing. The staircase and the hall remained dark.

And the glowing bar below the bedroom door was as bright as ever.

There has to be some reason for the light, I thought. *Maybe the bedroom window inside that room isn't boarded up, and it's letting in light from outside.*

No, that couldn't be it. It was too cloudy and rainy outside. The light coming from below the bedroom door had a yellow cast to it, like it was coming from a lamp or a ceiling light.

Regardless, there had to be *some* reason.

I walked slowly toward the door, not making a sound. Another crash of thunder boomed, and a gust of wind howled and groaned like a snarling lion. I could hear rain on the roof, and rain hitting the side of the house.

When I was right in front of the door, I stopped. I clicked off the flashlight.

At my feet, the glowing light from beneath the door was bright enough to illuminate my sneakers.

I leaned toward the door, listening for any movement. I heard nothing.

Slowly, ever so slowly, I reached out and grasped the doorknob. It was metal, and it felt cold in my hand.

I turned it. It jiggled a little bit, and then there was a light *thunk*. I pushed the door.

Instantly, the light went out! I didn't even have time to see where it had came from!

The door squeaked as it swung open, exposing nothing but darkness.

I quickly turned on the flashlight Dad had given me. The beam penetrated the darkness like a laser, and I swept it across the dark room.

There was nothing there.

That was kind of freaky. I knew that I had

seen a light coming from beneath the door.

I *knew* it.

Yet, behind the door, there was nothing but inky blackness.

I moved the beam back and forth through the room. It was totally empty. There was nothing in the room at all.

I reached around the wall and fumbled for the light switch. I found it, and clicked it up and down several times.

No lights came on. Except for the flashlight beam, the room remained cloaked in darkness.

I reached out and grasped the doorknob, slowly pulling the door closed. Its hinges squeaked as the door swung toward me, and made a loud *click* as it shut.

At that point, I was about to turn and leave. Maybe I just *thought* that I had seen a light. Maybe it was just my imagination.

But the moment the door clicked shut, I knew that I hadn't imagined the light.

Because it had returned!

At my feet, a light from beneath the door blinked on, once again illuminating my sneakers.

I immediately took a giant step back.

There was no mistake about it. There was a light on in that room. I was seeing it with my own eyes.

And what made me decide to open that door again, I'll never know. But I'll tell you this: what was about to happen would be the strangest — and scariest — thing that would ever happen to me in my whole entire life.

3

I slowly dropped down on my hands and knees, being careful not to bang the flashlight on the hard floor. My heart jackhammered in my chest.

Pound-pound-pound-pound-pound . . . .

Where was that light coming from?

I leaned over until my cheek touched the cold floor.

I peered beneath the door.

Now I was *certain* that there was a light on. Under the crack of the door, I could see the floor inside the room. I could see a tiny portion of the wall on the other side of the room, too.

There was no mistake. I hadn't been imagining things.

There was a light on in the bedroom.

I remained motionless, staring under the bedroom door through the thin strip of light. My mind raced.

Where could that light be coming from? I thought.

Thunder clapped outside and I jumped. The noise had surprised me.

I stood up slowly, quietly, all the while staring down at the thin strip of light that came from beneath the door.

Grasping the flashlight tightly, I clicked it on and took a step forward. I held my breath, reached out, and grasped the doorknob.

I waited there a moment, nervously looking at the light at my feet. Then I looked at my hand around the knob, then glanced back down at the bottom of the door.

The light was still on.

I took a deep breath, preparing myself. After all, I'm twelve. I'm not afraid of a strange light in a bedroom.

Am I?

I guess at the time, I wasn't sure. That's why I was hesitating.

I took another breath, held it, turned the knob quickly, and threw the door open. It spun on its hinges and smacked into the wall with a crash.

But the light . . . .

What happened next is difficult to describe.

There was a light in the bedroom, alright—*but it didn't seem to be coming from anywhere!* It was like a mist that swarmed around the room. When the door opened, the weird light-mist swirled like smoke and began seeping through the cracks of a boarded-up window, like it was trying to hide!

I did nothing but stare. I had never seen anything like this before in my entire life.

Within seconds, the light had disappeared, seeping through the cracks in the boards like water.

The room was dark once again!

I've seen television shows that investigate strange things that happen to people and places. Most of what I've seen can usually be explained by one thing or another. But I've read books about really odd things that happen without explanation.

That's how I felt right now. Like this was something out of a book.

Only it was *real*. It had happened to me. I had watched the light slither about the room and vanish like mist.

But . . . *hang on a minute.*

I trained the flashlight beam at the boarded-up window, and for the first time, I realized that I was shaking in my shoes. The flashlight trembled in my hand, and my knees shook.

Alright, Danielle, I ordered myself. *Get hold of yourself. There's a simple explanation for this.*

I held the light in one place, and the bright white spot lit up the boards that had been affixed to the wall.

Wait a minute, I thought. *That's not a window, after all.*

It was true. Now that I took a closer look, the boards were nailed from the floor to the ceiling. On the other wall, where more boards were affixed, they covered only enough space to fill the window.

But here, where I had watched the light disappear, the boards seemed to cover much more than a window.

The boards were covering up a door.

Why would someone board up a door? I wondered. *Where did it lead to? Was it a door that led downstairs? Or outside?*

I moved the beam of light around, exposing the boards and the far wall.

It was a door, I was certain. Behind those boards was a door.

Why?

I've always been curious. I'm always trying to find out how things work, why things work, and why things do what they do. I guess I just have a curious mind.

A curious mind that gets me into trouble sometimes. It's just the way I am, though. I just need to have answers.

I'm curious, that's all.

There's a saying that my brother is always repeating. He says *'curiosity killed the cat, Danielle. Curiosity killed the cat.'*

But I can't help it. I'm just curious. I like to know things.

And my curiosity about the strange, boarded-up door was about to land me in *big* trouble.

Why I didn't go and get my mom and dad I'll never know. Maybe I just wanted to investigate the door myself.

Whatever the reason, I found myself tip-toeing slowly across the bedroom floor, the white flashlight beam trained on the wall before me.

Outside, the wind cried. Thunder rumbled in the distance, and the rain dripped off the roof. It sounded like the storm might be passing.

I stopped a few inches before the wall. The

flashlight beam lit up the boards, and, sure enough, I was right.

There *was* a door boarded up. I could see the wood through the cracks of the boards.

Why would someone board up a door? I thought once again. *To keep people out? Why?*

I reached out slowly, and my brother's words echoed in my head.

Curiosity killed the cat, Danielle. Curiosity killed the cat.

My finger touched one of the boards. It was old and dry. I felt the edge of it and began to pry it with my fingers. It took some work, but after a minute or two I was able to wiggle the board loose. In another minute I had succeeded in grasping it with my hand and pulling it from the wall.

I pulled the board away, set it aside on the floor, and proceeded to work at another board. It, too, required some work, but after a few minutes I was able to pull it free. The board came away, and I placed it on the floor next to the other one.

Curiosity killed the cat, Danielle. Curiosity killed the cat.

I grasped another board. This one came away easy, and I placed it on the floor next to the other two.

Soon, all of the boards had been pulled away, exposing a large, wooden door. The handle had been broken off. Whoever had closed up the door really wanted to keep people out.

I tried to fit my fingers around the edge of the door to pry it open.

No luck. There wasn't enough room to get my fingers in the crack between the door and the frame. I tried to grab hold of the broken doorknob, but that didn't work, either.

I shined the light all around the door. Besides the fact that it had been boarded-up and had a broken doorknob, it looked like any other wood door.

But in the bright light, I saw something else.

Scratch marks.

On the face of the door were long, thin scratch marks, like someone had carved on the door with a knife.

I leaned closer, bringing the light near the door.

No, not scratch marks, I thought. *Letters. There's something written on this door!*

I leaned closer still to try and make out the strange markings.

"Danger," I whispered, reading the words quietly. *"Do not open door. Or else . . ."*

I drew back.

Or else *what?* The warning abruptly stopped with a long scratch that went all the way down the door. It looked like someone had tried to finish writing something, but couldn't.

Now I was *really* curious. Why would someone write such a thing? It was only a door. Maybe it went to a closet or another room. Or maybe it didn't go anywhere. I wondered if Dad and Mom had seen the door when they came to look at the house before they bought it.

I stared at the words carved into the door. It looked like someone had used a small knife to inscribe the warning. The scratches weren't very deep, and if you didn't look close, you wouldn't even be able to see them.

I was standing in front of the door, wondering why someone would go through the trouble to

30

write something on the door, then board it up . . . when all of a sudden I knew what had made the words in the wood.

And I realized it the instant I felt sharp fingernails clawing into my back . . . .

The sharp claws dug into my skin, and I spun and screamed at the same time. I whirled and flung myself against the wall, shining the light at my attacker.

"YOU!" I screamed.

In the flashlight beam, my brother Derek looked back at me, smirking. He was holding a fake claw hand!

"See what Grandpa got me for my birthday?" he said, holding the plastic hand up for me to see.

It was gross. It looked like a creepy monster's hand, with fake fur and long, sharp nails.

"You just about scared me to death!" I scolded.

"Maybe I can do better next time," he said smartly.

"What are you doing here, anyway?" I asked. "You're supposed to be at Grandma and Grandpa's house in Toledo all week."

"The week is already up, and they're dropping me off. Besides . . . they wanted to see our new house. I haven't even seen it myself."

"Well, you didn't need to sneak up on me like you did!"

"Why?" he asked, looking over my shoulder at the dark wall and closed door. "Are you doing something you shouldn't be?"

"No," I replied sharply. "I'm not. I was just—"

What, exactly, was I doing? I wondered.

"I was just curious, that's all," I finished.

"Looks like you're wrecking our new house, if you ask me," Derek replied. Even with the flashlight beam trained on him, he could see the pile of boards on the floor behind me.

He pointed to the door. "Where does that go?" he asked.

"I don't know," I replied, turning to face the door. "I was trying to get it open. Someone had boarded it up. And here—"

I reached out and dragged a finger over the scratched letters. "Someone wrote this in the wood."

Derek stepped next to me and leaned toward the door, reading the words out loud.

"Danger. Do not open door. Or else." He stopped reading and faced me. "Or else what?"

"You've got me," I said, shrugging. "I was just trying to figure that out when you came up and scared me."

"I did a good job, didn't I?" he sneered, holding up the fake hand.

I punched him in the shoulder. Not hard, but hard enough. He winced, but he kept looking at the door.

"Maybe it's just a closet," he said.

"But why would someone board it up?" I asked. "And why would they scratch a warning in the door?"

"Beats me," Derek said. He turned to walk away.

"You're not even curious to know what's behind it?" I asked.

"Nope," he replied, shaking his head. "I've got better things to do than waste my day staring at some door. It was probably someone's idea of a joke."

Derek is right, I thought. *Whoever lived here before probably did this as a joke.*

I turned to follow my brother out of the bedroom. He was walking down the hall, and I had just stepped out of the room when I heard a creak.

Then another.

I turned, flashed the light into the room we had come from . . . and my blood ran cold.

"Derek!" I whispered. *"Look!"*

Derek was just about to go into another bedroom when he turned around and walked back to where I was standing. He looked into the room.

The door that I had discovered . . . the one that

36

I had pulled the boards from . . . *was open!*

"Did . . . did you do . . . do that?" Derek stammered.

"How could I do it?" I replied. "I was standing right here!"

But it wasn't the open door that made us gasp in horror—it was what was beyond the door that made Derek and I tremble with fear.

The door had opened by itself!

It had opened by itself, and Derek and I stared at the strange sight.

The only way I could describe what I saw would be this:

Another world.

That's what it looked like! It looked like the door opened into an entirely different realm than the one we were in. Beyond the door was not another room, but another whole world altogether. I saw strange looking trees,

39

mountains, a blue sky, and clouds. It was as if we were staring into a strange painting of some sort, only I knew that what we were seeing certainly wasn't mere artwork.

"Are . . . are you seeing what I'm seeing?" I stammered.

"Uh . . . uh . . . huh," Derek stammered back. "Wh . . . what is it?"

I shook my head slowly. *"I don't know,"* I whispered. *"But it sure isn't a hidden bathroom."*

I began to tip-toe slowly across the floor, closer and closer to the door. Derek was behind me.

"How can this be?" he asked. "I mean . . . it's like the door goes into another country or something."

"Look at those trees," I said, raising my arm and pointing. "I don't think trees like that even grow on earth."

The trees were tall and had thick, silver leaves. Each leaf was about as big as my hand, and was as shiny as foil. The tree trunks were black, and they were huge. Much bigger than any tree that grew in Ohio!

The sky was a beautiful, rich blue. Wisping white clouds, like ghosts, hung high above the trees. In the foreground, just beyond the door, was a peaceful field of tall, sinewy grass. Farther off, miles away, majestic mountains sprung up from the earth. Their white-capped tops licked at the blue sky.

Mountains?!?! I thought. *In Ohio? It's not possible!*

But, as the saying goes, 'seeing is believing'. I knew I wasn't dreaming. Neither was Derek. We both were seeing the strange world on the other side of the door.

It was *real*. I didn't know how, but it was very, very real. As real as the floor beneath my feet. As real as the thunderstorm that still raged outside.

And yet, in this strange world that we were peering into, there wasn't a hint of a storm. From the glittering trees and the long shadows, it appeared the sun was shining!

I took another step toward the odd door, toward the strange world beyond.

Now I could even smell it! The scent was

41

fresh and clean, like a spring day.

I took another step forward. If I took one more step, I would pass through the doorway.

"You're not thinking what I think you're thinking, are you?" Derek asked.

I didn't answer.

"Danielle?" he asked again. "What are you thinking?"

I turned my head, but my eyes remained on the strange sight beyond the door.

"What do *you* think?" I asked.

"I think that curiosity killed the cat."

"You're always saying that," I replied.

"That's because it's true," Derek stated flatly.

"Don't you want to see what this place is?" I asked.

"No," he answered, shaking his head.

"Yes you do. You're just being a chicken."

"Am not!"

"Are too!"

"Am not!"

"Then let's go. Just for a minute. We'll come right back."

There was no sound from Derek.

"Well?" I urged.

"Only for a minute?"

"Only for a minute," I promised. "Come on."

I took his hand and drew a breath. Just then, Derek's words drifted through my mind.

Curiosity killed the cat, Danielle.

I ignored the thought, and took a step into the strange, weird world on the other side of the door.

The world was incredible.

In many ways, it was just like Ohio . . . fields, trees, rocks, blue sky, clouds. But in many other ways it was so very, very different.

For instance, the trees were so silver and shiny that they appeared to be made out of steel. A light breeze caused the foil leaves to shake, and the sound was like a thousand tinkling wind chimes.

And the grass we were standing in was odd,

too. It was waist-high and green, but each blade was as stiff as wire. Walking through this field would probably be very difficult, if not impossible—like walking through pudding. I took another step, and, sure enough, it was hard to bend the thick blades of grass.

"Where is this place?" Derek asked, his voice trembling.

"Got me," I replied slowly. *"It doesn't look like any place I've seen before."*

We stared for a long time. The sun was warm, and it felt like it was a perfect summer day—wherever we were.

"We must have gone through a door to another world," I said.

"That's impossible," Derek replied, shaking his head.

"Then how do you explain it?" I asked, pointing at the mountains in the distance. "There are no mountains like that in Ohio." I swung my arm and pointed at a tree. "Or trees like *that*," I insisted. "Somehow, we entered another world through the door."

"Well, wherever we are, we'd—"

"Stop!" I interrupted. "Do you hear that?"

"Hear what?" Derek asked.

"Listen!"

We both stood frozen, listening. At first, we didn't hear anything.

But then . . . .

"What's that?" Derek asked.

I heard the sound again. It was a heavy, murmuring rumble. Suddenly, the ground beneath our feet began to shake.

"Earthquake!" I shouted. "It sounds like an earthquake!"

Without wasting another second, Derek and I spun to escape through the doorway. I didn't want to hang around in this strange world to find out what would happen next!

But we were in for a surprise.

"Oh my gosh!" I shouted. *"The door! Where did it go?!?!"*

The door was gone! The only thing behind us was a field!

Wherever we were, we were trapped. *There was no way out!*

47

The rumbling beneath our feet grew louder, and the ground began to shake like crazy! It was shaking so bad that I thought I was going to lose my balance and fall!

"What . . . what in the world is going on?!?!?" Derek shouted above the loud rumbling.

In the next moment, we knew.

There was a movement across the field that caught our attention, and suddenly there were dozens . . . *hundreds* . . . of the strangest creatures

I had ever seen. They were stampeding like a herd of rampaging elephants!

But they were unlike any animal I had ever seen before in my life.

They were really huge—probably as big as giraffes—but they were all white and had horns on their noses like a rhinoceros. Their skin looked rough, like the skin of an alligator, and their legs were short. They had tails that snapped and twisted as the creatures ran. They looked like they might be part horse, part elephant, part rhino, and part alligator . . . all rolled up into one giant creature! Clouds of dust spun through the air, kicked up from the ground by the charging beasts. I thought that maybe they might be dinosaurs, except they didn't look like any dinosaur I had seen in any books.

And they weren't running toward us, which made me happy. I don't think I'd like to be in the way of these creatures! I'd be squished like a pancake!

"Holy cow!" Derek exclaimed above the thundering roar. "What are those things? Where did they come from?"

I didn't have an answer for any of his questions. I was just as confused as he was. I mean . . . we didn't even know where we were!

We stood, frozen, watching the beasts run. After a few minutes, the rumbling ceased and the herd thinned. After another minute, the animals were gone.

Derek turned and looked at me.

"Where in the world are we?" he asked.

"We're not," I replied. "We're not anywhere in the world. There's no world like this that exists. I have to be dreaming."

Derek reached out and pinched my arm.

"Ouch!" I exclaimed, pulling my arm back. "That hurt!"

"Nope," Derek said, matter-of-factly. "You're not dreaming. And neither am I."

Derek turned back around, and we both stared in the direction where we had seen the herd of creatures. The rumbling was gone, and everything was quiet.

"We have to find that door," I whispered. "We have to find our way out of here."

I turned and looked around. The silver trees

shimmered gently, and the shiny leaves clinked together like metal wind chimes. The long, thick grass beneath my feet was rigid and stiff, as if it were frozen solid.

And suddenly, I had a strange feeling. Derek must have sensed it too, because he turned slowly and looked at me. Then his eyes darted around.

"Danielle," he whispered. "Do . . . do you have the feeling of being watched?"

"Yes," I replied quietly. My eyes scanned the field and the trees. I saw no one.

"But there's nobody around," Derek said. "I don't see anybody or anything."

Still, I had the very powerful sensation of being watched. I felt as if there was someone, somewhere, watching our every move.

To my horror, I was about to find that I was right.

They were in the sky.

Creatures.

Beasts.

Bizarre animals that I could have never possibly imagined.

I gasped. I shrieked. Derek spun to see what was the matter, and he looked up.

And screamed.

They were . . . .

What were they?

They looked like gargoyles, only much, much worse. The creatures were a reddish-brown color, and they looked part human, part gargoyle, part—

Ogre. That's what they are! Ogres! Ogres with wings!

I've seen movies about ogres, but I never knew that they existed. I thought they were just made up by someone's imagination.

But I'll tell you this: the creatures circling above us were not created by anyone's imagination. They had large, pointed ears and big, round heads. They all looked like they were wearing the same type of ragged clothing, and none of them wore shoes.

I counted twelve of them, hovering high above like vultures. They were far away, so I couldn't tell for sure how big they were, but I knew that they had to be much bigger than me or Derek.

We stared up at the beasts. They were looking down at us, their enormous wings beating the air.

"I think we're in big trouble," Derek whispered, his head craned back.

Moments after he spoke, one of the flying

ogres broke away from the others. The beast tucked in its wings and began spinning down toward us, faster and faster, plummeting toward the earth like a diving hawk!

And his *face*.

I could see the look on his half-human, half-animal face. I could see his mouth open, exposing jagged, sharp teeth.

That was all I wanted to see.

"*RUN!*" I shouted, turning away and bolting. Derek followed, and we both began to run through the tall, wiry grass. I had no idea where we were going to go, but we couldn't just stand in the middle of the field and let that flying beast get us!

Running was difficult. The grass was stiff and strong, not like normal grass at all. It was hard to move my legs. It was as if the blades of grass were like the long bristles of a wire brush, and it felt like we were wading in thick mud.

"*Head for the trees!*" Derek shouted. He was right next to me, and he, too, found it difficult to move.

I managed a glance over my shoulder, and

immediately wished I hadn't. The creature was still coming at us . . . and so were the others! The rest of the flying ogres were dropping out of the sky, heading right for us!

"We're not going to make it!" I shouted. *"We won't make it to the trees!"*

The last thing in the world I wanted was those nasty creatures grabbing hold of me. I was going to do anything I could to get away, but I knew that my chances weren't very good.

And suddenly, when I saw a pair of eyes hidden in the grass, I knew that we were *really* in trouble.

Derek had spotted the creatures at the exact same time that I had.

"Danielle!" he shouted. *"Look out!"*

He tried to warn me, but it was too late. Right at my feet, a creature suddenly popped up from beneath the grass! Then another!

I knew that no matter what happened now, it wasn't going to be good.

The creature on the ground was tiny . . . no taller than my waist. He looked like a small man, or maybe . . . maybe—

An elf?

What a strange world this was!

But it was what was in the hand of the tiny man that surprised me. He was holding a small, golf ball-sized object. Without warning, he suddenly drew his arm back and threw the object at me! Then another creature jumped up from the thick grass and did the same!

I ducked and put my hands over my head. Whatever the small object was, it missed me and went sailing past. One of the creatures had thrown one at Derek, too, and he fell to his knees and tumbled into the grass, dodging the object.

This was a nightmare! Not only did we have to worry about the beasts in the air, but now we had to deal with little men on the ground throwing things at us!

The object whizzed past my head, just missing my ear. I couldn't be sure, but it looked like the small man had thrown a *buckeye!*

That's right! *A buckeye!* The buckeye tree is the official state tree of Ohio, and it has small fruit called 'buckeyes' that are small, round, and spiny.

Inside are four or five seeds. If you ever visit Ohio, you're bound to see buckeyes just about everywhere.

Suddenly, there was a loud explosion behind me, and a flash of bright light. I heard a loud squeal. Another small man popped up from the grass and threw a buckeye into the air.

Wait a minute! I thought. *They aren't throwing them at us! They're throwing the buckeyes at the flying ogres!*

I fell to my knees into the grass and turned around.

The air was filled with smoke! Whatever the small men had thrown, they must have exploded in the air!

And what's more, the flying ogres were retreating! They were flapping hard and flying back up into the sky, grunting and screeching and making an awful racket. I could tell that they weren't happy at all!

Whatever was going on, the tiny men had saved us. They had scared off the giant ogres.

I thought that we were safe. I started to think that maybe things would work out, after all.

Maybe the tiny men were our friends.

Until there was a loud popping sound, and suddenly a net sprang up from the ground. It covered Derek and I completely, trapping us within the strong mesh.

"Hey!" Derek shouted, waving his arms wildly. "What's . . . what's going on?!?!?"

We struggled to break free of the net, but it was no use. The harder we tried, the more tangled we became.

Maybe the small men weren't our friends, after all . . . .

Although we knew it was hopeless, Derek and I both struggled to get out of the net. But our efforts were in vain. The net was too strong.

We were captured.

Within seconds, we were surrounded by the small men. They were talking among themselves, speaking a strange language that I didn't understand. They were scurrying all about, picking up the net in their hands. More and more of the tiny men arrived, and they all began to pull on the net.

We were moving! They were dragging us through the field!

"Hey!" I shouted. "You'd better let us go right now! When my dad finds out about this, he isn't going to be very happy!"

The small men paid no attention to me. They just kept dragging us along, through the long, thick grass.

"Where do you think they're taking us?" Derek whispered.

"Got me," I answered, my voice shaky. I had been scared when the creatures had attacked us from out of the sky . . . but now, I wasn't sure what was worse.

The small men pulled and pulled. They dragged us through a dark forest, through steep valleys and hills. All the while, they spoke among themselves in their strange language. Once in a while, one of them would turn around and glance at us to make sure we weren't trying to escape.

And one thing was for sure: there was no way that we were in Ohio. There was no way. We've traveled all over the state, and I've never, ever seen a place like this before.

After a while, we came to the side of a large mountain. We stopped near the mouth of an enormous cave, and the small men began to unwrap the netting from around us! Soon, the net had been pulled away. Derek and I stood up. I brushed myself off and looked around.

The small men were just staring. They were looking at us like we were some kind of strange animal that they hadn't seen before.

I wondered if we should try and run, but where would we go? We had no idea where we were.

So, at least for the time being, we were at the mercy of our captors—and now, they were going to make us go into the cave!

The tiny men motioned us toward the dark tunnel. It was obvious that we would have to do what they said.

I was scared, but, then again, they *had* saved us from the flying ogres.

I just didn't know why they captured us, or where they were taking us.

Or *why*.

The tiny men began to lead us into the cave. I looked at Derek, and he looked at me. I could see the fear in his eyes. There was nothing we could do.

So, we began to walk, not knowing where we were headed.

Not knowing what was in store for us.

Not knowing *anything*.

But I'll say this much: what we'd experienced since we first walked through the door was *nothing* compared to what we were about to discover.

We walked into the cave, and darkness enveloped us. Within moments, it was so dark that I couldn't see anything at all. I could hear footsteps on the stone beneath us, so I knew that the small men were still around. But I was kind of nervous, not being able to see where I was walking.

"Derek?" I asked quietly. "*Are you still here?*"

"*Right here,*" he whispered back. "*I sure wish I knew what was going on. I hope that —*"

"*Wait!*" I interrupted. "*Look up ahead!*"

Far ahead in the darkness, I could see a faint point of light.

"It must be the end of the tunnel," Derek said.

As we walked, the light became brighter and brighter. Soon, I could see the shadows of the strange men walking all around us. They had been silent as we walked through the cave, but now they began chattering to one another.

When we were at the opening of the tunnel, I stopped and stared.

"Holy cow," Derek said.

It was a city! There was a valley below us, and in it was a real city, complete with houses and buildings and streets! We had emerged on the side of a mountain, and the city was below us in a wide, lush valley. I could see movement on the streets in the distance.

It must be an entire city of tiny people!

"Wake me up when this is all over," I heard Derek say.

"Nope," I said, shaking my head. "We're wide awake. It seems like a dream, but it's not."

Suddenly, the crowd of small men was moving again, and we set off down a thin trail that wound down the side of the mountain. We walked for a long time, and I kept my eye on the approaching city. I still couldn't believe what was happening to us.

We were led through the city to a large building made of pure white, glass-like stone. Then we were led inside. Our footsteps echoed as we made our way down a long corridor.

At a large door, the small men stopped. One of them pulled out a ring of keys, opened the door, and stood back.

All of the men looked at us. They wanted us to go through the door.

They waited. Finally, one of the men motioned with his hand, waving us through the door.

I didn't want to go. I knew that once we were inside, the door would close and we would be locked in. It would be our prison, and there would be no escape.

But there was nothing I could do. There was nothing Derek could do. True, we might have been able to outrun them, but then what? We had nowhere to go. This world was just too weird.

We had no choice. We had to do what they said.

I drew a deep breath, closed my eyes, opened them, stepped through the door —

And stopped.

I gasped.

Behind me, Derek gasped. He grabbed my arm. We both froze, staring, our eyes wide. Neither of us could believe what we were seeing.

It was a banquet hall!

Lit torches lined the walls of a gigantic room. Small people, dozens of them, both men and women, sat at the table and stood against the walls. They were all staring at us. Giant glass light fixtures, aglow with burning candles, hung from the ceiling.

There was a long table in the center of a great room. It was covered with flowers and silver plates and bowls.

And food!

There were dozens of dishes on the table, and the air was filled with the dazzling smells of delicious food. I have to admit, the scent of all of that food made me pretty hungry!

And at the far end of the table . . . .

A king!

There was a king seated at a throne! He was small, like all of the other people. He had a long, gray beard and wore a red and gold crown. His clothing was bright, with lots of sparkling colors. Both of his hands rested on the golden arms of the throne.

There were other people seated at the table, too. They were dressed like royalty in their fancy robes and gowns.

And everyone in the room was silent. You could have heard a pin drop.

Suddenly, a small man approached us. He was carrying a silver tray with a cover on top of it. He stopped in front of me and raised the cover.

On the tray was a single buckeye! Just like any buckeye that you might find on a tree in Ohio!

He held the tray before me, waiting. Did he

want me to eat the buckeye? Is that what he wanted?

Fat chance of that!

Again, he motioned toward me with the tray. He clearly wanted me to have the buckeye.

So, I picked it up and held it in my hand. It looked like a plain old buckeye. I've seen a thousand of them in Ohio. Buckeyes are poisonous to humans, but not to squirrels. A long time ago, native Americans used to use them to catch fish. They would grind the nuts into a powder, and pour it into small pools. The stunned fish would rise to the surface, and they were easily scooped up by hand.

After I picked up the buckeye, the small man turned and walked away.

Just then . . . the strange king at the other end of the table began to speak . . . *in English!* We could understand him perfectly!

"Welcome!" he bellowed out.

The crowd of small people seated around the table echoed the king. "Welcome!" they all said at the same time, all speaking perfect English. Then the king raised his hand.

"Welcome to the Kingdom of the Gnomes!" he said. "I am King Bantoor, leader of the land. We have waited a very long time for your arrival!"

Huh? What did he mean by that? How could they be waiting for us?

Derek snickered.

"What is it?" I whispered.

"That's a funny name for a king," he whispered back. I elbowed him gently in the ribs.

"Be polite," I scolded, *"or we might not get out of here."*

The king suddenly got up from his chair and approached us. Like all of the others, he was pretty short compared to Derek and I.

"You must be very tired," he said. "Tired and hungry. Come! We have prepared a feast for you!" He waved his hand at the table, and gestured toward two empty chairs.

This was all getting very confusing.

"Wait," I said. "Where on earth are we? Where is this 'Kingdom of the Gnomes? Who are you people?"

"Questions will be answered soon," the king answered. "For now, we eat. Come!" Again, he motioned for us to sit down.

I looked at Derek, and he looked at me. He shrugged his shoulders, and we stepped toward the table. As we did, everyone sitting at the table stood up. They were all watching us.

I stood by the chair, waiting. Then it occurred to me: everyone around the table was waiting for *us* to sit down!

I took a seat, and Derek did the same. Immediately, all of the other gnomes sat back down. I still had the buckeye in my hand, and I placed it on the table next to my plate.

And then: the food was passed around. Talking began, but it was once again that strange language that we couldn't understand. There was laughter and a lot of smiles. The gnomes looked at us, their faces beaming.

The food was just like food that we usually ate. There were lots of vegetables, and even meat that tasted like roast beef. Everything was delicious!

Finally, when we were finished with the meal, King Bantoor tapped his glass with his fork. The crowd fell silent.

"Friends," he began, "we are honored to have our guests at our table."

The gnomes broke out into applause and cheering. They were all looking at Derek and I.

"However," the king continued, "they must be a little confused. Now is the time to explain to them what is happening."

I thought that he was going to continue speaking, but instead, a gnome approached us. He drew a knife from a tray of silverware and placed it on the table in front of me.

"Slice the magical orb into two pieces," the king ordered.

Huh? Magical orb? What was he talking about?

"He must mean the buckeye," Derek whispered, leaning toward me. *"He wants you to slice it in half."*

Everyone was watching me as I picked up the knife. I held the buckeye on the table and carefully sliced it in half, wondering what the big deal was.

Oh, I found out why it was such a big deal, alright.

And one thing was for certain: I hadn't sliced open an ordinary buckeye . . . because what happened next was *amazing*.

Inside of every buckeye, there is supposed to be five or six seeds.

At least, that's what's *supposed* to be inside a buckeye.

Not this one.

When I sliced the small fruit in half, a strange, cloudy mist seemed to explode from it. It was like a thick smoke, and I flinched in my chair and dropped the knife. I heard Derek gasp.

Then I heard the voice of the king speaking.

He was telling us that it was okay, that we wouldn't be harmed.

By now, the smoke pouring out from the buckeye was so thick that I couldn't see anything. The table seemed to vanish, as did all of the gnomes seated around us. Everything quickly disappeared in the murky smoke.

But then:

Other forms began to appear! Forms in the mist, right in front of me! It was like watching a movie unfold all around Derek and I.

As I watched, frozen to my chair, a story began to take place. It was like we were getting a history lesson in the fog!

I could hear the king's voice, but he sounded distant. He began to explain what we were seeing in the mist.

"We are simple gnome dwellers," he began. "Our home has been a place of mystery and magic for many, many years. We have lived here, in peace, for a long time. It is a world that exists outside of your world."

As he spoke, I could see the entire city through the mist. Like I said: it was just like watching a movie!

"Not long ago," King Bantoor continued, "a strange creature invaded our peaceful land. They came from their own world, from their own dimension. They were searching for the Everlasting Tree of Magic."

Suddenly, I could see the creatures that had attacked us! In the mist before me, the creatures were swarming through the sky! They looked hideous. All through the city, the gnomes were running to hide, trying to get away from the terrible flying ogres.

The king continued speaking.

"The Everlasting Tree of Magic is a tree that has grown since the beginning of time. It cannot be destroyed. On one branch, the tree yields exactly twelve magical orbs. These fruits of the tree bear the most powerful magic in the universe."

As he spoke, a buckeye tree suddenly came into view through the mist. Just an ordinary, everyday buckeye tree. It seemed to be so close that I could reach out and touch it! I could see a few buckeyes dangling from the branches.

"The terrible creatures that attacked were searching for the tree, and the magical fruit that it bears. They want to use the fruit for wickedness. They have been searching your world, and they have been searching our world. They are using this door to go between worlds."

Suddenly, a door appeared in the mist.

I gasped.

Derek gasped.

My eyes grew wide, and I shook my head. What I saw was out of this world.

15

"*That's . . . that's . . .* " Derek stammered.

"*That's the door we came through!*" I whispered. "*The door in the upstairs bedroom of our new house!*"

The mist swirled around the very door that I had discovered behind the boards . . . the very door that we had stepped through!

Crazy, I know. But right now, I'd believe just about anything!

"The Everlasting Tree of Magic grows in your world," the king explained. "Although there are many trees that look like it, only one is the authentic tree. It is this tree that you must find. We have been waiting for someone from your side to come through the door to help us. You must find the tree and replenish our supply of magical orbs. It is the only way we can fight off the terrible creatures."

In the mist, the door began to fade away, and in its place, one of those horrible creatures returned.

"The ogres want the tree all to themselves. They want the magical orbs for bad things. Once they have them, they will never be stopped."

The ogre in the mist seemed to be only a few feet away, and he was really gross-looking. He was huge, and he had wrinkly, rough skin the color of rust. Sharp teeth protruded from his mouth. He had wings, but at the moment they were folded in, hanging down his back. The tips of his wings almost touched the floor!

I drew back a little bit. Even though I knew that the creature wasn't really there, I wasn't comfortable being so close to him like that!

"Many years ago," the king said, "the ogres attacked our small village. They succeeded in stealing many of our magical orbs. They used them to cast a spell over the door that allowed us to travel between our world and yours. Ever since, we have been trapped here. We cannot travel to your world to search for the tree. That is what *you* must do."

The creature before me began to fade away. The mist started swirling, spinning faster and faster like a white tornado. It spun around and around, until a tiny point of mist found the split buckeye. Then, within seconds, it had seeped into the pod! The two halves of the buckeye leapt together, sealing itself closed. There was no cut mark, no slice to indicate it had ever been cut by a knife.

I looked around. All of the gnomes were looking at Derek and I.

"So, you want us to go back to our world," I said, "find this 'Tree of Magic', and bring a bunch of buckeyes . . . I mean 'magical orbs' . . . back to you?"

The king nodded his head. "That is correct," he said. "There are only twelve magical orbs on the tree. You will find them all on the same branch."

"But what about the ogres?" I asked. "What if they find the tree after we find it?"

The king's eyes grew wide. "You must not let them know where it is. Never. *Ever.* If they find the Everlasting Tree of Magic and gather the twelve orbs, they will never be defeated."

"And what about those other creatures that we saw?" Derek asked. "They were huge . . . and they made the ground shake when they ran."

"Ah, yes," the king replied, nodding his head. "Wild deer. You have nothing to fear from them. Unless, of course, you are in their way."

"Deer?!?!?!" I exclaimed. "They didn't look anything like deer at all!"

"That's because the ogres fed them some of the magical orbs," the king answered.

Other gnomes around the table nodded their heads.

"And . . . and they changed into those creatures?" Derek asked.

The king replied by nodding his head, then speaking. "The ogres wanted to use the deer to ride upon. However, as you saw, their experiment didn't go as planned. So, instead, they used the magical orbs to give themselves wings. Ogres aren't very smart . . . but they can be very dangerous if they have magical orbs."

This was crazy. Absolutely nuts. Gnomes? Ogres? Magical orbs? Deer that are twenty feet tall and look like . . . like *what?*

Freaky.

I sure had a lot of questions, but I was too confused to even speak anymore. All I could think about were the things that we'd been shown in the strange mist.

"A long time ago," King Bantoor said, "someone from your world came to our world. We were hoping that they would help us. But they were frightened off by the ogres."

I remembered the warning that I had discovered on the door. It had probably been written by that same person!

"But what happens if we don't find the tree first?" I asked. "I mean . . . what happens if the ogres find the tree before we do? Then what?"

The room became deathly silent. No one moved. It seemed like everyone had stopped breathing.

"Well," King Bantoor began, "you do not have to help us. You can go home. We can show you the door, and you can go back to your world. Back home. You can forget about us."

He paused a moment, sighed, then continued. "You are our final hope. We only have a few more magical orbs left. If the ogres find the tree—"

A gasp swept through the crowd, followed by silence. The king shook his head.

"I'm afraid it will be all over for us. But there's more to it than that."

He stopped speaking again, and I watched, waiting for him to continue. And when he did, his words sent a shiver of fear from the top of my head to the tips of my toes.

What the king said was *horrible*.

The king spoke slowly, and his eyes glanced to me, then to Derek, then back to me.

"Once the ogres have destroyed our kingdom, they will move on. The magical orbs will make the creatures very powerful. The ogres will seek out and destroy other kingdoms . . . and your world will be next. Your world will come under attack, and there is no one . . . nothing you or anyone in your world can do to stop them. If the ogres find the Everlasting Tree of Magic, the entire universe will be in danger."

I couldn't believe what I was hearing! Just thinking about those ugly creatures flying through the sky, invading Ohio and everywhere else, gave me goosebumps.

I looked at Derek. He looked at me. Everyone in the dining hall was looking at us.

And, when it came right down to it, we really didn't have a choice. I mean . . . I didn't know much about the gnomes, but they seemed nice enough. I certainly wouldn't want them or their city to be destroyed.

And I didn't want Ohio to be destroyed, either!

Derek shrugged. "But where do we begin?" he asked. "We don't know anything about this 'magical' tree. There are buckeye trees all over Ohio. In some other states, too. How will we know which one it is? And what do we do when we find it?"

"You will know," the king said, "when you are close. I cannot explain it, but when you are in the presence of the tree . . . if you are anywhere near it . . . you will know."

The hall was silent once again, and everyone was looking at us.

"Will you help?" King Bantoor finally asked again. His voice was softer, pleading.

What else can we do? I thought.

"Yes," I replied, nodding my head. Derek didn't say anything, but he nodded his head, too.

A warm smile grew on the king's lips. Around the room, people relaxed and began to smile.

"Excellent!" the king exclaimed. "We must prepare. You must be on your way immediately. There is no time to waste."

The dining hall became a bustle of activity as the gnomes began to disperse. They began chattering in their odd language again, and I couldn't understand what they were saying. But they seemed to be happy.

"I hope we know what we're getting into," I said to Derek.

"I hope so, too," he replied.

But we didn't. I guess I didn't know what to expect, but what was about to happen would be the most bizarre experience of my life.

The king led us through the city and to a stone building on the other side of the town. We were escorted by a half-dozen gnomes who walked around us. It was a really weird feeling, being the tallest people in the city! All of the buildings were small, like over-sized doghouses. Except, of course, the huge banquet hall we had just emerged from.

We followed King Bantoor through a small door. Derek and I had to duck to get inside. The gnomes that escorted us remained outdoors.

We were in a small room. It was dimly lit with a single table in the middle. There were no chairs, no other items in the room.

The king reached into his robe and pulled out some strange looking keys. They jangled as he held them up.

"We must keep our magical orbs hidden at all times," he said, "just in case."

"Are they the same ones that you used to fight off the ogres when they were attacking us?" I asked.

The king nodded. "Yes," he said, inserting the key in what appeared to be a small hole in the wall. "Here, we keep the very last of our magical orbs."

Suddenly, a hidden door swung open. It wasn't very big, like a cupboard door. Inside was a small leather bag. The king pulled it out and set it onto the table. He pulled a drawstring and opened the bag.

Two buckeyes fell out. They looked like any one of the thousands of buckeyes you might see if you ever come to Ohio. They certainly didn't look like they were magical!

"These are the last two that we have left," the king explained, "except the one that you saw in the dining hall. These two, however, are very special. Among other things, they will allow you to become invisible. You will not be seen by any of the creatures in your world. The orbs can also help you in other times of danger."

Derek smiled. "You mean . . . I could be standing right next to my mom and dad . . . and they wouldn't be able to see me?" he asked.

The king shook his head. "When you use the orbs to make yourselves invisible, no one will be able to see or hear you," he said. "No one will know you are there. However, no one will be able to *help* you, either. And one more thing: because these orbs are very old, the magic contained in them will wear off after a short while. Once it wears off, the magic will be gone. You will not be able to use the orbs again."

Wow! That would be kind of cool! I'd always wondered what it would be like to be invisible. Now I was going to find out!

The king must have noticed our smiles,

because he frowned and spoke again.

"The only problem is that the ogres have traveled through the door. They are now in your world. They cannot be seen by anyone . . . yet. They will be invisible. However, as long as you have the orbs with you, *you* will be able to see them. If you use your magical orbs to become invisible, the ogres still will not be able to see you. Understand?"

Derek and I nodded.

"But if they discover that you are searching for the Everlasting Tree of Magic," King Bantoor continued, "they will do everything they can to stop you. They will—"

King Bantoor was interrupted by frantic yelling and noises from outside. We could hear gnomes yelling and shouting in panic.

The small king rushed past us and looked out the door.

"They're here!" he cried, looking up into the sky. *"The ogres! They're attacking!"*

Derek and I ran to the door to look, and I did not like what I saw.

At *all*.

The sky was filled with ogres! There were dozens of them, swooping down from the clouds. They were screeching and screaming . . . and they didn't look very happy.

"They know you are here!" the king said, ducking back into the room. "Quickly! We must hurry!"

"Where?!?!" I asked. "Where do we go?!?!?"

"You must follow me! Come!"

And with that, King Bantoor did an amazing thing.

He disappeared!

The king vanished!

Well, not really vanished. But he was gone so quickly that I wasn't sure what had just happened. King Bantoor had simply crawled into the tiny space where the magical orbs had been stored!

I peered into the hole, but saw no sign of him.

"Ummm . . . Mister . . . uhhh . . . king? Are you there?" Outside, I could hear the panicky

97

shrieks of the gnomes as they ran from the invading ogres.

Suddenly, I could see the king's head! He was so small that climbing into the tiny place had been easy.

"Come quickly!" he said. Then he pulled back and was gone again.

"How are we going to get through there?" Derek asked.

No reply.

Outside, we could still hear a lot of commotion. I was sure that the ogres must be getting close.

Did they know that we were here? If they did, we would be goners for sure!

"If only we were smaller," Derek said. "Then we could slip through that hole really easy."

Instantly, a strange thing began to happen. I began to feel really weird, like . . .

Like . . . .

Like I was getting smaller!

Derek could feel it too!

"Hey! What's . . . what's going on?!?!?" he said.

Before we knew it, Derek and I had *shrunk!* We were now no bigger than the gnomes themselves, but our clothes were still the same size! It looked like we were wearing clothing that was ten sizes too big!

"Wow, do you look funny!" Derek said to me.

"You don't look so handsome yourself," I shot back. His clothes, like my own, were too big to fit him. They looked baggy and bulky. His shirt sleeves hung past his hands like two elephant trunks.

"Come on!" I urged. "Maybe now we can escape!"

I reached my arms into the hole in the wall and pulled myself through, falling onto a hard, sandy surface. Derek was right behind me . . . and it was a good thing, too, because one of the ogres was trying to get into the building! I could hear the creature screaming and howling behind the door on the other side of the room.

Suddenly, King Bantoor was at my side, and he helped Derek through. Then he reached in and slammed the small door shut.

We were safe — at least for the time being.

But we still were half of our normal size!

"How do we change back to our normal size?" I wondered aloud.

It was like I had spoken the magic words. In the next instant, I had that real funny feeling again. I felt my body changing, growing larger and larger. Derek did, too, and within seconds, we were both back to our normal size.

"Ah, yes," the king said. "You are learning how to use the magical orbs already. That is good. They will serve you well."

"But we didn't do anything," I said.

"Oh, but you did," King Bantoor replied, nodding his head. "The orbs that you carry can sense what you need and when you need it. In a way, they can read your minds."

"Cool!" Derek whispered. *"I'd really like a hot fudge sundae!"*

I shook my head. "You're a ninny," I scolded. "How can you think of sundaes at a time like this?"

"Easy," he shrugged. "I like sundaes."

I looked around. We were in a large underground tunnel.

"Follow me," the king said. "Because of the ogres, we have built these caverns all over beneath the city. They give us a place to hide, at least for a short while. I will lead you back to the door to your world."

"But it disappeared," I said, remembering what had happened when we tried to return through it.

"Ah, yes, but only while the ogres were around in this world. You see, they may have used magic to keep us from going through the door to your world . . . but we used magic to make the door disappear. It made it difficult for them to find their way into your world. Now, however, all that is changed."

I wasn't quite sure what he meant when he said that 'all that is changed' . . . but we were about to find out.

We walked through the dark tunnel. It was hard to see, and Derek kept bumping into me. The king, however, seemed to know exactly where he was going. We followed the sound of his footsteps and soon, we could see a small pinpoint of daylight up ahead.

When we reached the small opening, King Bantoor knelt down, peering out into the bright sunshine.

"All clear," he said.

I leaned forward and looked outside. Silver trees towered up into the sky, and in the distance, I could see the mountain range. It looked like we were at the exact place where we had started from.

Derek leaned forward and looked outside. He raised his hand to his forehead, shielding his eyes from the bright sun.

"Where is the door?" he asked, scanning the field.

"It is in the same place that it always has been," the king replied.

I looked harder, but I couldn't see a thing. I felt as if I was looking into one of those 3-D posters with lots of color and squiggly lines.

"Do you see it?" King Bantoor asked.

Derek and I shook our heads.

"No," Derek replied. "How are we going to get out of here if we can't even—"

"Derek! Look!" I interrupted, pointing. "There's something! Right over there!"

It was true! The door seemed to be appearing right before our eyes!

What's more, it looked just like it did from the

other side. It looked like someone had put a closet door right in the middle of the field.

"You see?" the king replied. "That is how the magical orbs work. There are many other things that they can do, too. You will find out very soon that the orbs are very, very powerful."

I reached into my pocket and pulled out the buckeye, holding it in the palm of my hand. It was hard to imagine that there was anything magical about it. After all, I'd seen hundreds of them before.

But maybe King Bantoor was right. Maybe there was some 'Everlasting Tree of Magic' somewhere in Ohio.

"I don't see any ogres," Derek said.

"You must be careful," the king replied. "Just because you don't see any, doesn't mean that they are not around. Now . . . you must go."

"But . . . but what do we do?" I stammered. I wasn't really thrilled about this whole thing. "What if we get attacked by ogres? What do we do when we find the tree?"

"You will know what to do," the king answered. His gray beard swished as he bobbed his head "Just use your magical orbs. They will lead you to the tree. You will know what to do when you find the tree. And the orbs will help you."

I hoped he was right.

"Let's go," I said. I was really looking forward to getting back to our new house and seeing Mom and Dad again.

We squirmed through the small opening. King Bantoor remained inside the tunnel, in the shadows.

"Good luck," he called out, and vanished into the darkness of the cave.

Derek and I walked toward the door, struggling through the thick, strong grass. The door sure looked strange, sitting there in the field like it was. There were no walls around it, no windows, no *nothing*.

Just a door.

While we walked, I looked around nervously, searching for ogres. Thankfully, we didn't see any . . . not yet anyway.

But we were about to.

Derek and I reached the door at the same time. It opened easily, and I stepped through first, followed closely by my brother. Within seconds, we had left the strange world behind. Now we stood in the gloomy darkness of the upstairs bedroom of our new home.

Home.

We had made it. We were back in Ohio.

I heaved a sigh of relief.

"Did that just happen?" I asked Derek.

He raised his eyebrows, then dug into his pocket and pulled out the buckeye.

"Yep," he said, flipping the small fruit into the air and catching it in the palm of his hand. "We were there, alright."

"What do we do now?" I asked.

"You've got me," he answered, looking around. "Everything looks the same. I don't see any magical tree."

"Duh," I said. "We're supposed to find it. I don't think we're going to find it growing inside the house."

"Well, let's go find Mom and Dad and let them know where we've been," Derek said. "They've probably been looking all over for us."

I didn't know what we would tell Mom and Dad when we found them. I mean . . . we couldn't tell them that we spent the last few hours in a different world! They'd think that we'd both gone bonkers!

I could hear rain and wind outside. The storm had gotten worse. Thunder rumbled, shaking the entire house. Wind howled.

We walked out the bedroom, down the short,

dark hallway, and down the stairs. I could hear the shuffling of feet somewhere in one of the rooms. Mom and Dad and Grandpa and Grandma were probably wondering where on earth we were.

Derek glanced at his watch.

"Danielle!" he exclaimed, raising his wrist. He held his arm up. *"Look!"*

"Yeah?" I said. "It's three-twenty. Big deal."

"It was three-twenty when I came up to find you!" he said. *"No time has gone by at all!"*

I stopped on the stairs, grabbed his wrist, and looked at his watch again. Closer this time.

"What?!?!" I gasped, my eyes widening. "Are you sure?!?!"

He nodded. "Positive. I looked at my watch when I was coming up the stairs. It was three-twenty. But now . . . ."

"It's still three twenty!" I finished. *"No time has gone by at all!"* I let go of his arm.

"Things just get stranger and stranger," he said. "I wonder what is going to happen next."

"I don't know," I replied, shaking my head. "But remember what the king said. He said that there are ogres in our world now, looking for the Everlasting Tree of Magic."

And that was when a scream suddenly rang out through the house. It was loud and shrill, and it echoed through the empty rooms and halls.

And we knew instantly who it was.

Mom!

Mom's scream made Derek and I jump. We looked at each other, our eyes wide.

Something awful had happened. I'd never heard Mom scream like that before.

Ever.

We bolted downstairs, following the sound of Mom's shriek. I could hear other noises, too . . . like Dad's footsteps as he rushed to help Mom.

I sprang down the hall with Derek right behind me.

What's happening? I wondered. *Is it an ogre? Is Mom being attacked by an ogre?!?!?!*

I know that the king had said that no one would be able to see them except Derek and I, but now I wasn't so sure.

At the end of the hall I flew around the corner, stopping instantly. Derek slammed into my back. We were both out of breath.

Mom was standing on a chair. She had a look of terror on her face, and she was pointing at something on the ground, near a corner. Dad was leaning over, trying to see what Mom was pointing at.

"I tell you, I saw it!" Mom shrieked. *"It was right there!"*

"Saw what?!?!" I asked frantically. "What did you see?"

"A mouse!" Mom said, her voice trembling. "It was right there, in that corner!" She thrust her finger toward the corner.

Derek nudged me, and I elbowed him back.

"She freaked because of a mouse?" he snickered. I elbowed him again.

"Well, maybe it was a big *mouse,"* I replied

112

sharply.

"Yeah," Derek snickered again. *"With giant fangs and claws and — "*

I elbowed him again. *"It's not fair to make fun of her,"* I whispered. *"Especially not after what we've seen today."*

Derek was silent, and we stood in the doorway, watching Mom point at the corner. Dad had picked up a magazine and rolled it up. What he was planning to do with it, I'll never know.

But Derek was right. The whole scene was pretty funny. I'll never forget the sight of my mom standing on a chair, her eyes wide, pointing at the corner like there was a monster coming after her.

"Maybe it went into another room," Derek said, turning. "We'll go look for it."

"Where did Grandma and Grandpa go?" I asked.

"They're outside, looking around the yard," Dad answered. He pointed out a window that he had taken the boards from. I turned, and I could see Grandma and Grandpa outside in the backyard, walking slowly. They each had an umbrella to shield themselves from the driving rain.

But most importantly, I didn't see any ogres.

I turned and followed Derek as he walked down the hall. He started giggling, and I pinched his side.

"Be nice," I said.

"I can't believe that Mom is afraid of mice," he replied, shaking his head.

We walked into the kitchen. There were boxes piled up everywhere—on the counter, on the floor, even on the dining room table. Moving in was going to be a big job.

But of course, we had a big job ahead of us. We had to find the Everlasting Tree of Magic before the ogres did.

"I don't even know where to begin to look for that silly tree," I said to Derek. "The king said that the buckeyes would lead us there. I don't know—"

Suddenly, I realized that Derek wasn't listening to me. He was frozen, staring across the living room at something. I peered over his shoulder to see what he was looking at . . . and I froze like a statue.

It was an ogre! *Inside our house!*

A *huge* one!

He was standing on the stairs, his head moving from side to side, like he was looking for something.

"Duck down!" I whispered frantically, and I quickly darted behind a pile of stacked boxes. Derek followed and he bumped into me, almost knocking me over.

We peered around the boxes and stared at the huge beast on the stairs. He was still looking around, up and down and all over.

Searching.

Then, he looked right at us . . . and I knew right then that we were in a mess of trouble.

What now? I wondered.

My heart drummed. My blood froze. I felt cold all over.

The ogre was strange looking. He looked almost like a ghost, and, as I watched, I realized that he had a transparent quality, like I could see right through him. He still looked like the other ogres that we had seen in that freaky world, but his color had faded.

Derek and I didn't move a muscle. The ogre

looked away, and then looked back toward us.

He hadn't spotted us, after all!

We remained perfectly still as the huge creature glided down the stairs, slowly, very slowly, without making a sound. His wings were folded neatly behind his back, so we couldn't see them until he turned sideways.

For as big as he was, I thought that he would make an awful racket . . . but he made no sound at all. And as he moved, his ugly head bobbed around, searching, looking for something.

I hoped he wasn't looking for us!

It strode slowly into the living room, and now we could see just how big he really was. The beast actually had to duck its head down to keep from bumping into the ceiling!

After looking around for a few moments, the animal—if you could call him that—turned and looked out the window. I could see its huge wings folded behind him. Still, the creature had a strange, glossy look to him. He looked like he could just disappear into thin air.

"I don't think he knows we're here," I whispered over Derek's shoulder.

"Oh, he knows we're here, alright," Derek whispered back. "He can sense us. Maybe he can smell us. But he hasn't seen us."

The creature turned and passed through the kitchen. Derek was right . . . the creature probably knew that we were here . . . but he hadn't seen us!

The ogre passed the refrigerator, then stopped for a moment.

He turned his head and sniffed the air.

Then he began to walk down the hall.

Toward the room where Mom and Dad were!

What would happen? What would happen when the creature went into the room where Mom and Dad were? Would the creature be able to see them? Would Mom and Dad be able to see the creature?

Derek tip-toed across the kitchen floor, and I followed. We both leaned forward, peering down the hall.

The creature was only a few feet away, and he was walking right toward the room where Mom and Dad were.

"Well, I don't see him anywhere," I heard Dad say. "Are you *sure* you saw a mouse?"

"Of course I'm sure," I heard Mom reply. "I know what a mouse looks like, and I saw one in that corner."

"Well, I'll have to get some mouse traps later today. That will take care of them."

Just then, Dad came through the door and into the hallway! He was right in front of the ogre . . . but neither beast nor human saw one another! At least, if the ogre saw my dad, the creature didn't seem to care too much.

Dad looked up and saw Derek and I staring out from behind the boxes.

"You two look like you've seen a ghost," he said. "Really . . . it was only a mouse. It's nothing to be worried about. You don't have to hide."

Great. Now Dad thinks that we were hiding from a mouse!

He walked right past us, and then Mom came out of the room. She, too, walked right past the ogre without even seeing it!

"I'll tell you," she said. "Having a mouse in

the house is like having a monster in the house."

"You're . . . you're right about that," I stammered as Mom walked past.

"And what are you two doing?" she asked, looking down at us. "There's lots of work to be done. Don't just stand in the hall like you've seen a ghost."

But Mom didn't understand. We hadn't seen a ghost . . . we'd seen an ogre.

And something told me that an ogre was a lot worse than a ghost.

Then, without warning, the ogre stormed away from us. He approached the front door of the house.

With its huge, wart-covered hand, it reached out and opened the door. In an instant the beast had slipped outside, into the rainy afternoon. I could hear the rain fall on the porch, and the wind howling through the trees outside. Dad did, too, and he walked over to where we were standing, looking curiously at the open door.

"Hmmph," he said. "The wind must've blown the door open. Will you go close it, Danielle?"

Dad walked back to the table and I walked slowly down the hall. Thoughts whirled in my brain like a flock of birds, and I knew that Derek and I had gotten in way over our heads.

I reached the door and peered out into the rain. I stuck my head out, craning it around, looking to see where the ogre might have gone.

I looked to the left. No ogre.

I looked to the right. No ogre.

I looked down the street, around parked cars and houses.

No ogre.

I looked down on the ground to see if I could see any footprints.

There were none. It was like he had simply vanished.

But then I looked up . . . and when I saw the giant arm coming down, reaching for me with sharp, curved claws, I knew there was no chance of escape.

He had been hiding on the roof of the porch, and now it was too late for me to do anything.

Instantly, I was yanked from the ground and up into the air! The ogre was using his powerful wings to hover just above the roof, and he easily snatched me from the doorway.

Derek saw what was happening and he rushed to help.

"Mom!" he shouted. "Dad! Grandpa! Anybody! Help! Danielle's in trouble!"

I knew that my parents were going to freak when they saw what was happening, but I didn't care. I didn't want to be carted away by a giant, slimy, over-grown warthog!

I was kicking and screaming as the ogre dragged me up onto the roof. Suddenly, I felt a hand grasp my ankle.

"Hang on, Danielle!" he shouted. *"I won't let him get you!"*

Problem was, the creature already *had* me! He was holding my arm so tight that I thought it was going to break!

"Don't let go!" I screamed. I figured that if he could hold on just a few more seconds, Mom and Dad would be here to help, too.

But suddenly, I felt Derek's grasp slipping.

"No!" I shouted. *"Don't let me go!"*

"I . . . can't . . . can't hold on much longer!" Derek shouted back.

I began beating the creature's arm with my fist, but I think it did nothing except make him even more mad.

I felt Derek's hand slip. He couldn't hold on any longer.

I could hear the ogre's wings beating the air, and he was making weird grunting sounds as he pulled me higher into the sky. The creature and I were a couple of feet above the roof now.

Just when I thought that things were hopeless, I remembered the buckeye in my pocket.

With my free hand, I reached into my jeans and was relieved to find the magical orb. I pulled it out, clenching it tightly in my fist.

But how would I use it? I still didn't know how the thing was supposed to work. All I knew was that it had magical powers.

"I wish you would let me go right now!" I shouted.

All of a sudden, the ogre let me go! He made another grunting sound, and he released his grip. I fell to the edge of the roof with a heavy *thud!* and then I tumbled sideways—and fell over the edge!

Oh no! I had succeeded in getting away from the ogre . . . *but now I was going to fall off the roof and break my neck!*

I fell.

The most I could hope for was a broken leg. I was bound to get hurt pretty bad. I figured that if I fell from the roof and only got a broken leg, I'd be pretty lucky.

Thwaak! Thud!

I tumbled to the grass in a heap. My elbow banged on the cement patio, but it didn't hurt too bad. I didn't even break my leg like I thought I would! Actually my landing wasn't bad at all.

And in the next second, I knew why.

"Oof!" I heard Derek exclaim. His voice was strained and hoarse. "Get . . . off . . . me!"

I had landed on Derek! I had landed on Derek, and he had broken my fall!

I rolled off of him. We were both soaked to the skin by now, and the wet grass didn't help much.

I looked up into the sky. Gray clouds hung like wrinkled sheets, and rain poured down.

The ogre was gone!

Derek followed my gaze. "Where did he go?" he asked, getting to his feet.

"I don't know," I replied, still searching the sky. The ogre had vanished . . . or so I thought.

Suddenly a noise came from the side of the house.

Derek and I stood in the falling rain, listening.

Squish. Squish-squish.

Footsteps.

I took a step back, and so did Derek.

Squish-squish . . . .

There would be no time to run inside. We would have to stay and fight.

All of a sudden, Grandma and Grandpa rushed around the corner beneath their umbrellas!

Derek and I let out a sigh of relief. At that exact moment, Mom came to the door.

"What were you two yelling about?" she demanded. "And why are you standing outside in the rain? Look at you! You both look like drowned rats!"

"Mom, you wouldn't believe me if I told you," I said.

"You're right, I probably wouldn't. Get in here this instant and get dried off."

I looked at Derek, and he looked at me. We both knew that it would be no use trying to explain to Mom. She'd think that we were just making up a story.

"Um, did anyone see that big bird in the sky?" I asked.

Grandma and Grandpa looked at each other and shrugged.

"Not us," Grandma said. "I didn't see any bird. Did you, Dear?"

Grandpa shook his head. "Nope. I didn't see a bird."

"Come on, you two," Mom repeated. "Get in here and get dried off."

I got to my feet and followed Derek into the house. Mom walked down the hall and went back to work unpacking things in the kitchen. When she was out of sight, I turned to Derek.

We are in big trouble, I whispered.

"Tell me something I don't know," he replied. "How in the world are we going to find that tree without being eaten alive by one of those ogres?

We have no idea where to begin to look, and those creatures could be anywhere."

"And no one can see them except for us," I said. "If we tell anyone that there are flying ogres in Ohio, they're going to think we've lost our marbles."

I was still holding the buckeye in my hand. It was hard to imagine that it was actually magical.

"What we need is a map," I said, turning the buckeye over in my hand. "A map that would lead us to the Everlasting Tree of Magic."

Just then, I heard Dad's voice coming from the kitchen. "Well, I'll be," he was saying. "That's strange. *Very* strange."

Derek and I walked down the empty hall and into the kitchen where Mom and Dad were. They were both staring at something on the counter.

"What is it?" Derek asked.

"I'm not sure," Dad replied, glancing up at us. "It was folded and stuffed in between the cupboards. It—" he picked up a large piece of paper. I could see the creases in it from where it had been folded. "It looks like it's some sort of map."

Derek and I looked at each other, stunned. Then I glanced down at the buckeye in my hand. I had just mentioned that we needed a map . . . and all of a sudden, Dad had found one!

This was getting stranger and stranger by the minute.

"Can I look at it?" I asked Dad.

He handed the paper to me, and I held it out for Derek to see.

Oh my gosh! I thought. I looked at Derek. He looked at me.

We both looked at the map. All we could do was stare.

The map was drawn in pencil, and appeared to be very old. The paper was yellowed with age.

And it looked like it had been drawn by a kid, too. There were roads and buildings that had been marked, and a compass drawn in the right hand corner that pointed north. There was a drawing of our new house . . . and even an 'X' where the door upstairs was!

But right in the middle of the map was—
A tree!

It was a buckeye tree, that was for sure. I could tell by all of the spiny buckeyes that had been drawn in among the leaves.

And right beneath it, these words were scrawled:

EVERLASTING TREE OF MAGIC

"Can I have this, Dad?" I asked.

Dad shrugged. He hadn't paid too much attention to the map.

"Sure," he said. "But we need both of you guys to dry off and start unpacking your things. Have you two decided who is going to have which room?"

"Not yet," Derek piped in. "We were just going to go and do that. Come on, Danielle."

I snatched a small flashlight from the counter and followed Derek upstairs. I picked the room on the left, and he picked the room on the right. Neither one of us wanted the room with the strange, disappearing door!

"Let me see that map again," Derek asked. I

pulled the map from my pocket and spread it out on the floor in my empty room. I clicked on the flashlight.

"This thing will lead us right to the tree!" I exclaimed. "Look!" I pointed to the map and placed my finger on the paper. "Here's our house right here." I moved my finger across the paper. "And here are the houses across the street. There is a river over there, and a park. The tree is inside that park! This is going to be easy!"

"Let's go right now!" Derek said, his voice bubbling with excitement.

I shook my head. "It's getting dark. Besides—it's still raining like crazy. We'll have to wait until tomorrow."

But there was one thing I hadn't thought of.

Maybe the ogres wouldn't wait for us.

Maybe they had other plans.

I was about to find out that very night.

For dinner, Dad picked up a pizza from a restaurant a few blocks away, and we all ate on folding chairs in the living room. Afterwards, we said good-bye to Grandma and Grandpa, and they headed back to their home in Toledo.

The rest of the evening was spent unpacking boxes and setting things up in my bedroom. We'd all be using sleeping bags that night, since the moving van wasn't supposed to arrive until the next day. That's when all of the furniture would get here.

A man from the power company came out and turned on the electricity, and we finally had lights.

Later that night, after I climbed into my sleeping bag, I stayed awake for a long time. I listened to the wind and rain, and thought about all of the weird things that had happened that afternoon. I wondered if, when I woke up the next day, I would discover that it all had been a dream.

No, I thought. *What happened today was no dream. No dream at all.* I rubbed my sore elbow, remembering my fall from the roof.

Not a dream, for sure.

And to think . . . those ogres could be *anywhere!* Just the thought of one of those ugly things made me cringe. I saw a movie about an ogre and a donkey, and the ogre was actually kind of cute.

Not these ogres. These ogres were ugly with a capital 'U'!

I kept my magical buckeye with me that night, just in case I needed to use it. I had no idea when an ogre might show up.

And as it turned out, I wasn't going to have to wait very long . . . because in the next instant, a huge shadow appeared at the door of my bedroom!

The shadow came over me like a black ghost. I cringed and grasped my buckeye tightly in my fist, wondering what to do.

Was it an ogre? If it was, then what? Could I use the buckeye to just 'wish' the creature away? I was still unsure as to how to work the magical buckeyes, anyway. So far, I'd considered ourselves pretty lucky.

Now, with an enormous shadow filling my bedroom door at night, I shuddered to think that my luck had run out.

Then:

The shadow moved!

"Who . . . who's there?" I stammered, my voice choking with fear.

A light clicked on, and I was overcome with relief.

It wasn't an ogre, after all! It was *Mom!*

"I just came up to check on you," she said.

"You just about scared me to death!" I replied. "I didn't know it was you."

"Sorry about that," she said, clicking off the light. "Sweet dreams. See you in the morning." I heard her slippers softly pad away on the wood floor. She peered into Derek's room, then walked down the stairs.

Still, I was pretty nervous and had a hard time falling asleep. I knew that those ogres could be anywhere, at any time. I would be glad when this whole thing was over with.

I rolled the buckeye over in my hands, gripping it firmly, knowing that it would be my only defense against the awful creatures. After a lot of tossing and turning, I was finally able to fall asleep.

It was sometime later when I was awakened by a creaking on the floor. I lay in my sleeping bag, frozen stiff, too afraid to move.

Was it Mom checking in on me again?

Was it Dad?

Or Derek?

It was very dark in the room, and it was difficult to see.

Suddenly, there was a shadow in my doorway, and I heard another loud creak.

And a deep, growling groan.

This time, it wasn't Mom.

It wasn't Dad.

Or Derek.

This time, it was an ogre . . . and he was right here in my bedroom!

30

Suddenly, I woke up and breathed a huge sigh of relief. Whew! I hadn't been awake . . . I had only been dreaming!

I turned my head and looked at the dark doorway.

No ogre, no shadow, no nothing.

Boy, was I relieved!

I rolled over and yawned, and snuggled deeper into my sleeping bag. Soon, I had fallen back to sleep.

When I awoke again, the sun was up. The boards were still on the windows, but I could see sunlight streaming through the cracks. The storm had finally passed. I stretched, got up and dressed, and went downstairs.

No one else was around. Mom and Dad were already up, but they were gone. They had left a note on the counter saying that they had gone to the grocery store and then to the hardware store, and would be home soon. Derek was still sleeping.

I was hungry. The fridge was nearly empty, but I found a slice of pizza from the night before, and I ate it cold. It was yummy! I love cold pizza.

And then I looked out the window.

I stopped chewing, and froze.

Ogres.

Not one, not two — but dozens of them! They were in the yard, and in the trees. Some of them were in the sky.

And they were all looking this way. They were looking at our house. Maybe they were looking at me!

I turned, sprinted across the living room,

bounded up the stairs, and flew into Derek's room.

He was still fast asleep, and I shook his sleeping bag.

"Derek!" I hissed. *"Derek! Wake up! They're here!"*

Derek's eyes opened, and he blinked a couple times.

"Wha . . .wha . . . who's here?" he stuttered, gently wiping his eyes with his fists.

"Ogres!" I exclaimed. "They have our house surrounded!"

That woke him up right away. He leapt from his sleeping bag and both of us bounded down the stairs.

"Where?!?!?" he asked, as we sailed into the living room.

"Look!" I cried, pointing out the window.

Derek gasped when he saw all of the ogres outside. They knew that we were here, alright. They knew that we each had magical orbs. And *they* knew that *we* knew where the Everlasting Tree of Magic was.

And that's what they wanted.

"Hang on," Derek said, flying back upstairs. "I've got to get out of my pajamas!"

He returned after a moment wearing jeans and a red sweatshirt.

"What now?" he huffed. "Now what do we do?"

I didn't say anything for a moment.

Think, Danielle, I ordered myself. *Think. Use your head. Use your brain.*

"Well, we have to get to the tree before they do, so we have to do it without the ogres knowing about it. Somehow, we have to sneak past them."

We thought about it for a long time, all the while keeping a watchful eye on the ogres that surrounded our house. On the street, cars went by. No one paid any attention to the ogres.

How could they? No one could see them but us!

And suddenly, remembering what King Bantoor had told us, I had an idea.

"I think I've got it!" I exclaimed excitedly. "I think I know what we can do!"

When I explained to Derek, his eyes grew.

"That just might work!" he said. "Let's try it!"

And with that, I pulled out the buckeye that was in my pocket, and Derek pulled out his.

"Are you ready?" I asked.

"Let's give 'er a whirl!" Derek said. "I'll bet this is going to be cool!"

I grasped the buckeye tightly in my hand, closed my eyes, and spoke.

"Magical orbs . . . I want you to make Derek and I . . . *invisible!*"

Nothing happened — at first.

My heart sank, and I could tell that Derek was disappointed, too.

But within a few seconds, I began to feel very strange.

"Danielle! You're . . . you're—" he was pointing at my arm.

It was vanishing! My arm was vanishing!

And so was my foot! And my leg! Derek was disappearing, too!

Within a few seconds, we were both invisible!

"This is cool!" I heard Derek's voice say. But I couldn't see him! He was standing right next to me, but he was completely invisible!

I looked down at myself . . . or I *tried* to, anyway. I couldn't, because I was totally invisible, too!

"These buckeyes are awesome!" Derek exclaimed. "Maybe we can keep a couple after we take them back to that other world."

That would be cool! I sure would love to have my own magical buckeye that I could use . . . especially if I could make myself invisible anytime that I wanted!

But right now, we had other things to worry about. Just because we were invisible didn't mean that we were safe. We had no idea what kind of powers that the ogres had.

We were about to find out.

"Come on," I said. "Let's see if the ogres can see us."

I walked down the hall and opened the front door. There were ogres on this side of the house, too.

When the door opened, they all looked.

But I didn't think that they could see me. I think they saw the door opening, and that was it. They couldn't see Derek and me.

"Are you still here?" I whispered.

"Right here," Derek replied quietly. His voice was close by.

"Okay," I whispered. *"I'm going to go out into the yard. Stay here, and keep the door open so I can run back inside if I need to."*

I can't tell you how weird it is to be invisible. When I looked down, I couldn't see my body. I couldn't see my arms. It was like I wasn't even there!

But most importantly, I could tell by watching the ogres that *they* couldn't see me!

I turned and waved for Derek to come toward me, but obviously, I couldn't see him.

Duh, I thought, shaking my head at my own thoughtlessness. *How can I wave Derek over? I'm invisible, too!*

I walked back to the porch, and bumped into Derek.

"Ouch!" he whispered. *"You poked me in the gut!"*

"Sorry about that," I replied quietly. *"I didn't see you. And neither can the ogres! We're completely invisible!"*

"Do you think we can make it past them without them knowing?" Derek asked.

"I think we can, if we —" I stopped speaking and pointed, but then I remembered that Derek couldn't see my arm. *"Look!"* I said. *"Someone is coming!"*

A man was jogging by. He ran right in front of the ogres, and they didn't pay any attention to him! The jogger didn't see the ogres, either. He just ran on by, huffing and puffing. Soon, he went around the corner and was gone.

It was really weird how the ogres could exist in another dimension, and not be seen by anyone except Derek and I!

"Come on," I whispered. *"Let's be quiet and walk right past them. Hang on to my hand so we don't lose each other."*

It was hard finding Derek's hand! Being invisible sure was cool, but it certainly had its share of problems!

We walked, hand in hand, down the driveway

and across the street. We walked right past a few ogres, and they never even saw us! They just looked toward our house, like they were waiting for us to come out!

This was going to be easier than I thought. All we had to do now was to find the tree in the park and take a bunch of buckeyes back to the gnomes. It would be a cinch.

At least, I thought it would be . . . until I looked down and saw part of my shoe.

Then part of my leg.

And my arm.

Oh no! The magic was wearing off! We weren't invisible anymore . . . and there were ogres all around us!

Derek noticed it at the same time I did.

"Danielle!" he whispered frantically. *"It's . . . it's wearing off!"*

I dug into my pocket and pulled out the buckeye.

"Invisible! Make us invisible again!"

Nothing happened!

"I . . . I think that the magic is gone!" I said. "I think it's all used up!"

Now we *were* in trouble. The king had warned us that the magic in the buckeye wouldn't last long, and he was right.

Suddenly, one of the ogres spotted us! He let out a loud grunt, and caught the attention of the other ogres.

"Run!" I screamed.

Derek and I took off, running across the street and behind a house. I didn't even look back. In my mind, I could see the map, and I knew that the Everlasting Tree of Magic couldn't be far. It was in the park. It was in the park, and we had to make it there first.

Before the ogres found it.

I didn't know what we'd do when we reached it, but I figured that if we found the branch with the magical buckeyes, then we could use them against the ogres. Maybe we could throw a couple of them and they would explode in a cloud of smoke, scaring off the ogres.

I could hear the beasts behind us. Some of them were running, and I could hear the sound of flapping wings as some of them took to the air.

"Faster!" I screamed. "We have to find the tree!"

We darted around houses and over fences,

and right through someone's garden.

"Look up ahead!" Derek suddenly cried. "Up there! In the park!"

I glanced ahead. In the middle of a big field stood a large buckeye tree! And part way up the tree, there was a branch—

with buckeyes on it! There were no other buckeyes on the tree, except for that single branch!

"That's it!" I shouted. "It has to be! We can make it!"

I glanced behind me to see how far away the ogres were. The ones that were in the air were the closest, and I was sure that we would be able to make it to the buckeye tree before they caught up with us.

And then, at the worst possible time, I fell.

I had just turned my head back around and was still running as fast as I could, but I caught my foot on a small bush—

—and tripped.

Instantly, I was sent flying, tumbling into the grass, head over heels. I rolled to a stop, jumped back to my feet, and began to run again . . . but it was too late.

A large arm suddenly clasped my shoulder, and then another around my waist.

"Derek!" I screamed.

Derek stopped and turned around.

"No!" I shouted. *"Get to the tree! You can't stop the ogres without the magical orbs!"*

Suddenly, I was pulled up into the air! I struggled to break out of the ogre's grasp, but it was no use.

And let me tell you . . . I was *terrified.*

But I had another fear, too.

What if the ogres discovered the tree? What if they found out that it was the Everlasting Tree of Magic?

What then?

The ogre was carrying me higher into the sky. I could see Derek below me, running frantically toward the tree. There were ogres right behind him!

"Run, Derek, run!" I screamed. He was almost to the tree.

"Faster!" I urged. *"There's one right behind you!"*

And there was, too.

It was gaining quickly, and in the next instant it was easy to see that Derek wouldn't make it. The ogre was just too fast.

In the next moment, my worst fear came true. I heard my brother scream as the giant ogre lunged.

He was attacking Derek!

Suddenly, Derek disappeared as the huge beast tackled him.

We were goners. We both had been captured before we had reached the tree. Now, not only were Derek and I at the mercy of the ogres, but the Kingdom of the Gnomes would be destroyed.

And then, of course, they would never be stopped.

I closed my eyes, and waited for the worst.

33

I was totally helpless, and my brother was, too. I was being carried off by a huge ogre, and Derek had been tackled by one before he could reach the Everlasting Tree of Magic.

I didn't know what would happen, but I was sure that the ogres now knew where the tree was.

And I knew that the Kingdom of Gnomes would be destroyed.

I heard an ogre screech, and I looked down. *Derek was standing up!*

He was standing up, and he was holding a buckeye in his hand! The ogre that had attacked him was backing up, like he was afraid of Derek!

Derek backed up, closer to the tree. The ogre kept backing away.

I couldn't figure out what had happened. Just a second ago, the ogre had tackled Derek.

Now, Derek was standing up to the ogre! Whatever he had done, it had worked.

Other ogres had arrived, and they surrounded the tree. Derek was trapped, but the ogres wouldn't come any closer.

"Stay back!" I heard Derek shout! *"Get back! Now!"*

The ogres obeyed him!

Somehow, he had found a magical orb, and he was able to use the magic!

"You! Up in the sky!" he commanded. *"Let my sister go!"*

It was the wrong thing to say, of course, because the ogre instantly released his grasp from around me. In the next instant, I was tumbling through the air in a free fall, spiraling toward the ground!

"Derek!" I screamed as I fell faster and faster toward the ground.

"Hang on!" Derek shouted.

Suddenly, I was overcome by a strange feeling. My whole body felt lighter, and I had the strange sensation of slowing down —

And I was!

I was no longer plummeting toward the ground. Instead, I slowed to a near stop. I was floating and drifting gently, like a feather in the wind.

I caught a glimpse of Derek. He was standing beneath the tree, holding the buckeye in his hand like he was pointing it at me. The ogres had formed a large circle around the tree — but they weren't coming any closer.

"You're doing it!" I shouted. I was floating, weightless, through the air, drifting over the ogres toward Derek.

"Only a few feet more!" I exclaimed.

It sure felt weird to be suspended in the air with nothing holding me.

In seconds, I was back firmly on solid ground again. I don't think I have ever felt more relieved in my entire life!

I looked around and behind me, and counted twenty ogres glaring at us. We were surrounded, but they were keeping their distance.

And man . . . did they ever look *mad!* Their eyes glowed with a burning fury, and I could tell that they were angry because we found the Everlasting Tree of Magic. We had found it, and now, there was nothing that they could do.

Or so I thought.

I turned around to speak to Derek, and horror gripped me like a vice.

An ogre had been sneaking up on him! Derek had no idea that he was there, and the beast was towering up behind him — *ready to attack!*

There wasn't even time for me to shout.

In an instant, the beast was upon Derek. He went flying forward as the ogre tackled him, and the magical orb went flying into the air.

I didn't waste any time. Before the buckeye even landed on the grass, I sprang for it. I had to grab it before any of the ogres did.

Plus, I had to keep the rest of them away from the tree. If even one ogre got hold of one of those magical buckeyes, it would be all over for us — and the Kingdom of the Gnomes. Not to mention the fact that the ogres would also be powerful enough to take over Ohio . . . and maybe the whole United States! The thought of these hideous beasts swarming all over made me run even faster.

The buckeye hit the ground and bounced to a stop. There were several ogres coming, all of them trying to get the magical orb that lay in the grass.

I dove, reaching my hands out in front of me like I was diving into a swimming pool.

Out of the corner of my eye, I could see an ogre leap forward. He was going for the buckeye.

But I got there first.

I snatched up the magical orb in my hand and started to roll away through the grass. The ogre crashed to the ground right behind me . . . empty handed.

I leapt to my feet, swinging my arm wildly, displaying the buckeye in my hand.

"Back!" I shouted. *"Get back! Get away or I'll turn you all into little mice!"*

All of a sudden, the ogres stopped in their

170

tracks, frozen. They all had weird looks on their faces. Even the ogre that had attacked Derek was looking at me with its head turned.

And suddenly —

The creatures began to change! They began to change into . . . .

Into —

Mice!

It was unbelievable! Right before our very eyes, the huge ogres began to twist and change. They shrank, and their wings and arms and legs seemed to seep into their bodies. Fur began to sprout through their skin!

And then, seconds later:

Mice.

That was all that they were. Harmless mice, scurrying about in the grass, running as if they had no place to go.

"Danielle!" Derek exclaimed. "That was awesome!"

"Well, it was kind of accidental," I said, looking at the buckeye in my palm. "Gosh . . . these things sure are powerful."

The ogres had been reduced to nothing more

than harmless mice. They were scurrying this way and that, scrambling about like little wind-up toys gone mad.

I looked at the buckeye in my hand, then looked at Derek.

"We have to get these to the gnomes," I said, glancing up into the tree that towered above.

Derek scrambled to his feet and snapped his head around, watching the tiny mice scurry away.

"Man, it was a good thing I found that buckeye when I fell," he said. "I landed right on top of it."

So that's what happened!

When the ogre attacked Derek, he had landed on a buckeye that must have fallen from the tree!

"Come on," I said. "Let's get the rest of them and take them to the gnomes. I'm sure that there are more ogres around."

"Yeah, but now that we've found the tree with all of these magical buckeyes, the ogres can't hurt us," Derek replied.

He was wrong. He was very, *very* wrong—as we were about to find out.

35

Collecting the buckeyes was easy. I'm really good at climbing trees, and I scrambled up the trunk and onto the limb that had the eleven remaining magical orbs.

I pulled them from the branches like apples, and dropped them down to Derek. He made a pouch with the bottom of his shirt and carried them.

"That's all of them," I shouted down to him. He double-checked by counting all the ones he had in his pouch.

"That's twelve," he shouted up to me. "We've got 'em all."

I scrambled back down the tree and walked up to Derek. We both spent a minute just staring at the buckeyes that we had gathered. It seemed so strange that they were so powerful, yet they looked like everyday, normal buckeyes.

"Come on," I said. "The sooner we get these to the gnomes, the better."

We walked through the park, around several blocks, and finally made it back to the house. All the while, we kept a close eye out for more ogres. We didn't see any.

Nor did we see our car parked in the driveway. Mom and Dad were still gone.

And when we went inside the house, an eerie feeling crept over me.

I felt like I was being watched.

"*Derek,*" I whispered, stopping in the hall. "*Do you feel like someone is watching you?*"

Derek looked around. He shook his head.

"Nope," he replied. "You're the only one watching me."

"Do you think it's possible that there could be ogres inside the house?" I asked.

"I don't care if there are," he replied. He reached into the pouch of his shirt and held up a buckeye. "With these little babies here, I'm not afraid of a hundred ogres." He tossed one a few feet in the air with his free hand, and it landed in the pouch he had made by stretching the bottom of his shirt. "It sure would be cool to keep a few of these for ourselves."

"Yeah, and you'd do nothing but get into trouble," I said, rolling my eyes. "Come on. Let's go back through the door and take the buckeyes to the gnomes."

Our footsteps echoed down the empty hall. When we reached the living room, I looked around suspiciously. I couldn't help but have the feeling that we were being watched.

We went upstairs and into the room with the secret door.

It was open!

It had opened by itself, just like it had yesterday. On the other side, I could see the same strange world.

But the feeling of being watched was so powerful that I shuddered.

"You don't feel that?" I asked Derek. My voice trembled.

"Feel what?" he replied. "I don't know what you're talking about. Come on."

He walked toward the door, and I was about to follow, when a noise behind me caught my attention.

I whirled around.

I froze.

I gasped.

And I screamed.

36

Behind us, in the hall, was an ogre.

He had been hiding in *my* bedroom! He had been waiting for us!

When I screamed, the ogre suddenly charged.

Derek heard my shout and turned around just as the huge ogre slammed into us. I was knocked against the wall, and Derek was sent flying through the door and into the other world.

And the magical orbs in his shirt-pouch went flying. They spilled out into the air and tumbled into the thick grass.

The ogre immediately chased after Derek, and his huge body filled the doorway. He was so big he had a hard time trying to fit through.

I sprang into action. If that ogre was able to get his hands on just *one* of the buckeyes, we would be in a lot of trouble . . . and so would the gnomes.

I sailed through the door into the other world, ready for anything, ready to start picking up the spilled buckeyes. I saw Derek, and he was already picking up the orbs that had scattered in between the long blades of grass.

But the ogre was right behind him!

"Derek! Behind you!" I shrieked. Derek dove to the side and rolled into the thick grass.

Suddenly, I saw movement in the grass near the ogre.

A gnome!

He had a buckeye in his hand and he drew it back. He let it fly, hurling the orb like a baseball.

The ogre tried to get out of the way, but it was too late. The buckeye struck the creature directly in the forehead. The orb bounced off and vanished into the thick grass.

And the beast froze—and I mean *froze!* In a split-second, the ogre had turned into an ice statue!

Suddenly, there were gnomes everywhere. They were coming out of holes in the ground, running around, scooping up the orbs that Derek had spilled. Soon, they had found all twelve.

The king appeared, and he walked up to Derek and I. He was smiling, and he extended his hand. He shook hands with Derek, and then with me.

"You did it!" he exclaimed. "You have saved our kingdom! We are forever grateful to both of you."

"Hey, piece of cake," Derek said, shrugging. "We're glad we could help."

"You must stay for a feast," the king insisted. "We must reward you and repay you for your help."

I looked at Derek, and he looked at me. It sounded like it would be fun, but I decided against it. After all . . . what would happen if Mom and Dad came home and came to look for

179

us? Would they find the door and travel into this world, too?

"We would love to," I said, "but we have to return to our world. We have people there that are expecting us."

"Yeah, like our Mom and Dad," Derek added. "They're going to be home soon. I'm not sure that they'd be real happy if they found out we were traveling to some other world."

"I understand," King Bantoor replied.

By now, all of the other gnomes had gathered around. Some of them were talking in their strange language. One of them leaned toward the king and whispered something.

"Splendid idea!" the king exclaimed. "Please give me one of the magical orbs!"

One of the gnomes handed him a buckeye, and the king held it out.

Was he going to give it to us to keep?!?! That would be awesome!

The king bent down and picked up a stone. He clasped both of his hands together, holding both the buckeye and the stone. Then, after a moment, he opened his hands, extending the rock toward us.

"The magical orb is too powerful for you to have in your world," he began. "However, I have placed a small amount of its magic in this stone. I think that you might find it useful."

I reached out and took the rock in my hand. It looked like an ordinary rock . . . just like you'd find anywhere.

"Thanks," I said, rolling the stone over in my hand. I wondered how powerful it would be, and what kind of magic it could be used for.

"How will it work?" Derek asked. "I mean, we never even figured out how to use the buckeyes . . . I mean . . . the magical orbs. The magic just seemed to happen."

The king nodded. "That is why it is so important that we have them with us in our kingdom. We are the only ones who know how to use their magic. The orbs are far too powerful for anyone else to use. Especially ogres. But you will find out how to use your stone. Do not worry." He smiled.

I turned and looked at the door behind us, then turned and faced the king again.

"Well, we'd better go," I said, nudging Derek. "Mom and Dad are going to be back here any minute."

We said goodbye to the king and the other gnomes, turned, and stepped back through the door.

When we were in the bedroom, we turned back around. The gnomes were watching us.

Suddenly, the door began to close. It swung shut with a loud clunk, and Derek and I were all alone.

But then something else began to happen.

"Danielle!" Derek exclaimed. He was pointing at the closed door. *"Look!"*

37

The door we had just passed through began to *vanish!*

We watched in amazement as the door began to blend in with the wall around it. In less than a minute the door was gone. Derek and I were staring at nothing but a blank wall.

I stepped forward and placed my palm on the place where the door had been.

Nothing there. There was no door, no nothing.

Just the wall.

"That was just too freaky," I said, shaking my head.

"Let me see that rock," Derek said.

I turned and handed it to him. He held it close to his face and stared at it. "I wonder what it can do," he said.

"Try something," I said.

"Okay."

He thought for a moment, and then his eyes caught fire. He smiled a wide grin.

"I wish I had a million dollars," he said.

I rolled my eyes.

Nothing happened. We waited and waited. I wondered if maybe a bag of money might magically appear.

Nope.

"So much for the magic rock," Derek said. He handed it back to me. "You try it."

I held the stone in my hand, looking at it. I closed my eyes. "I wish I had a penny."

"A penny?" Derek said. "What can you buy with a penny?"

"Well, maybe the magic isn't strong enough to

get a million dollars," I said. "I thought a penny might be more practical."

We waited. I didn't know what to expect, which was a good thing . . . because nothing happened. No penny fell from the sky. Nothing appeared instantly in front of us.

"What good is a magical rock if we can't make it do any magic?" Derek asked.

"You've got me," I replied. "The king said we would find out on our own, though. Maybe it's—"

I stopped speaking.

"What is it?" Derek asked. "What?"

I had been looking at the rock, when all of a sudden something appeared in the stone! I drew the rock closer for a better look—and I couldn't believe what I saw!

"What is it?" Derek repeated.

"It's . . . it's the kingdom!" I exclaimed. "I can see it in the rock!" I held the rock up for Derek to see.

Sure enough, I could see the Kingdom of the Gnomes. It was faint, like we were looking into a crystal ball, but there was no mistake.

"Maybe that is what the stone is for," I said. "Maybe it is for us to keep so that we'll always remember what we saw when we were there."

Derek frowned. "I would have liked a million dollars a whole lot better," he said.

Well . . . that's my brother for you.

●●●

And so, our strange adventure with the ogres came to an end. In my diary, I wrote down everything that happened so I wouldn't ever forget. The strange door, the weird world, and the tree.

I showed the special stone to my mom one day, and asked her if she could see anything.

"No," she said, rolling the stone over in her hand. "What am I supposed to see?"

"Oh, I was just curious," I replied. Apparently, Derek and I were the only ones who could look into the rock and catch a glimpse of the Kingdom of the Gnomes.

Over the summer I returned to the Everlasting Tree of Magic many times to find buckeyes. Once in a while, I would hold one of the buckeyes in my hand and try to do some magic.

It never worked. All of the magical orbs are now with the gnomes, safe in their world.

And that's probably a good thing.

Later that year, during the December holidays, Mom, Dad, Derek, and I went to Florida for vacation. We go there for two weeks every winter, and we always have a blast. Last year, we went to Disneyworld in Orlando. This year, we went to Tampa, on the other side of the state. Compared to Ohio, Florida is really warm in the winter!

We stayed at a place right near the ocean, and I went to the beach every day. One afternoon, I met someone about my age walking near the shore. He was carrying a can of pop and a Frisbee.

We began talking, and he told me that his name was Justin, and that he lived in Tampa. He said that Florida is a lot of fun, all year round.

I told him that we had fun in Ohio, too.

"Does it ever get foggy around there?" he asked. I thought it was kind of a strange question.

"Yes," I said, nodding my head. "Sometimes. Why?"

"You wouldn't believe me if I told you," he said, shaking his head.

"Believe what?" I asked. "You mean to tell me that you never have any fog in Florida?"

"Oh, we have fog alright," he said. "It's just that . . . well . . . I just don't like fog, that's all."

I looked at him. He looked . . . *frightened.*

"Why don't you like the fog?" I asked. "What's wrong with it?"

"It's not the fog itself that I'm afraid of," Justin replied. *"It's what's in the fog that scares me."*

Huh? What on earth did he mean?

"What's in the fog that's so scary?" I asked, shrugging my shoulders. "Fog is just that: fog. It's just a cloud."

He shook his head from side to side. "Oh, no it's not," he insisted. "There are places here in Florida where there are things *in* the fog."

"In the fog? What are you talking about?"

He looked around warily, then looked at me.

"Phantoms," he said hesitantly. "There are phantoms in the fog. I'll tell you about what happened to me if you promise not to tell anyone."

"Promise," I said.

I have to admit, it was hard to believe. But I sure wanted to hear about it!

"Okay," Justin replied. He sat down in the sand, and I did, too.

"It all started with the hurricane," he began.

I listened as Justin told me what he had been through.

The sun that day was very, very, hot . . . but the story that Justin told me chilled me to the bone.

next in the

AMERICAN CHILLERS

series:

#3: FLORIDA FOG PHANTOMS

turn the page to read a few spine-chilling chapters . . . if you dare!

Before I even start to tell you this story, you have to realize something:

Florida is a cool state.

I love Florida. It's my home. I've lived here my entire twelve years.

My little sister, Maria, loves Florida.

And my Mom and Dad. We *all* love Florida.

So, when I tell you what happened to me, I'm not doing it to scare you.

I don't want you to be frightened or afraid.

But I think you will be.

Matter of fact . . . I *know* you will.

And if you ever get a chance to come to

Florida, you'll have fun. You'll have an *awesome* time.

Just beware of the fog.

Beware of the fog phantoms.

I'm not sure . . . but they *could* come back.

They might even be here now. Waiting.

Waiting . . . *for you.*

I suppose I should start at the beginning. Last summer. Right after the hurricane.

That's when weird things started to happen.

✚ ✚ ✚ ✚

We all knew there was a storm coming. We heard about it on the radio. The TV weatherman told us all about it.

It was a hurricane. You may have even heard about it or read about it, because it was the strangest storm of the year.

Not the biggest.

Not the worst.

The *strangest.*

My name is Justin Martinez, and I live in a city called Tampa. It's a city on the western side of

194

Florida, right next to the ocean. A lot of people come here to visit, because there are a lot of things to see and do. We even have a professional football team called the Tampa Bay Buccaneers.

And Tampa happened to be in the direct path of Hurricane Alice. That's right. They give names to all of the hurricanes and tropical storms that we have, and this one they called Alice.

In 1992, a hurricane named Andrew caused twenty *billion* dollars in damage.

Hurricanes aren't anything to mess around with.

Two days before Hurricane Alice arrived, everyone in the city began boarding up their houses. Stores, shops, buildings . . . everyone boarded up their windows to protect against the high winds and heavy rains. Many people . . . including our family . . . stayed at a hotel in another city until the storm passed.

Tuesday, the storm hit just as expected. However, we were a long ways away, so we didn't have any problems.

On Wednesday, we went home. The storm hadn't damaged much, after all. It had been listed as a category 3 hurricane, which is pretty severe. However, by the time it reached land, it had dropped to a category 1, which is the lowest ranking. A category 1 can still be dangerous, though. Some of the streets around our neighborhood had been flooded, but by the time we made it home, most of the water was gone.

Everyone was thankful. A hurricane can do a lot of damage, but this time, the city was spared.

Or so I thought.

Because that night, a strange fog settled in all over the city. It was as thick as cream, and just as white. It was so thick, I could barely see the streetlight in front of our house. I had never seen fog so thick. It was kind of —

eerie.

Now, I'm twelve, and I'm not afraid of the fog.

But later that night, after I went to bed, something happened that made every single hair on my head stand straight up on end.

I was just about to go to bed when the phone rang. It was Caitlin McCalla, my neighbor across the street. Not only is she my neighbor, but she's also a good friend. She's really smart, too, and she helps me with my math homework.

"Have you seen Princess?" she asked. She sounded worried.

"No, I haven't," I replied. Princess is her dog. She's a Great Dane, and she's huge.

"She ran off a little while ago. She's never done that."

"I haven't seen her," I said. "But I'm sure she'll come back."

"I hope so. I'm kind of worried about her. Can you believe this fog?"

I kept the phone pressed to my ear and looked out the window. The fog was as thick as ever. I couldn't even see any lights on in Caitlin's house across the street!

"It's really weird," I replied. "The weather guy on TV said that it was because of the storm. He says that people shouldn't drive their cars until the fog lifts."

"I'm glad the storm wasn't a real bad one," she said. "This fog is bad enough. I hope that Princess isn't—"

All of a sudden, there was a loud *click* on the line, followed by crackling static.

Caitlin was gone.

"Hello?" I spoke into the telephone. "Caitlin? Caitlin?"

No answer.

I hung up the phone and picked it back up.

There was no dial tone.

I hung up the phone and went into the living room. Mom and Dad were watching television.

"The phone isn't working right," I said.

Dad turned. "I think it's because of the screwy weather," he replied. "It's doing some strange things all over the city."

I walked down the hall and into my bedroom. I left the light off and walked to the window.

Outside, the fog covered everything like a blanket. I tried really hard to see Caitlin's house across the street, but I couldn't. The only thing I could make out was the haunting, dim glow of the streetlight.

I yawned and climbed into bed, then I turned on the light on my nightstand. I like to read before I go to sleep. I'd been reading a ghost story, and I was almost finished with it.

I opened up the book and started to read.

The next thing I knew, the book was face down on the covers.

I had fallen asleep reading!

I closed the book and placed it on the table next to my bed, then reached up to turn the light off.

It was then that I heard a faint creaking sound. *Creeeeeeeeeeeak . . . .*

I froze. The sound was faint, but it had been

close.

Real close.

There were no other sounds in the house. It must have been late, because I didn't hear the sound of the TV on. Mom and Dad must've gone to bed.

And suddenly—

Creeeeeeeeeak . . . .

The noise sent a shiver down my spine.

Slowly, very slowly, I turned in the direction of my bedroom door. My hand still grasped the switch on the lamp, ready to turn it off.

But I wasn't turning the light off until I found out what had made that noise!

Without moving my head, I looked out the window. The fog was as thick as ever.

I looked back toward my bedroom door, and my entire body went stiff.

Creeeeeeeeeak . . . .

The sound was coming from the door! My bedroom door was opening . . . *all by itself!*

I couldn't breathe.

I couldn't move.

My heart clanged in my chest.

Creeeeeeeeak . . . .

The door kept swinging open, slowly, slowly, ever so slowly . . . .

Creeeeak . . . .

I just knew that there would be some hideous form behind my door pushing it open. It would have long fangs and claws and beady eyes.

And it was coming for me.

I knew it.

Creeeeeeeeeeak . . . .

And suddenly . . . .

I could see it! I could see a small piece of something white, standing in the hall!

It was a ghost!

It was . . . it was . . . .

"Justin? Are you awake?"

My sister?!?!?!?!

I heaved a giant sigh of relief. It was only Maria. She stood in the doorway in her nightgown.

"Sorry I scared you," she said.

"Who? Me?" I replied. "I wasn't scared. Not at all."

"I am," she said, her voice quivering. "I'm scared a lot."

I looked at her. She was trembling.

"What's wrong?" I asked.

"There's . . . there's something in the fog," she said.

She glanced out my bedroom window, and I did the same.

Heavy, white mist swirled just beyond the glass. The streetlight glowed, illuminating the fog like a giant, wispy ghost.

"There's nothing in the fog," I replied. "You were having a nightmare. Go back to bed."

And with that, I turned the light off, rolled over in bed, and closed my eyes.

I heard footsteps on my bedroom floor, and then I felt Maria's hand on my shoulder. She shook me gently.

"Justin," she said, "I saw something out there in the fog. It was moving. Some kind of creature. I'm scared. I really, really am."

I rolled over and turned toward her.

"There's nothing in the fog," I insisted angrily. "Go back to bed and quit bugging me!"

She drew her hand back from my shoulder, but she didn't move. She just stood there and sniffled.

Great, I thought. *I'm going to make her cry.*

Maria is a few years younger than I am. She can be a pest sometimes, but she's pretty sweet. I guess I kind of felt bad that she was scared.

And I was making it worse for her.

I sat up, swung my legs to the floor, and stood up. I took her hand in mine.

"Listen, Maria," I said. "There's nothing in

the fog. You were dreaming. I'm sure you were. Come on."

I led her by the hand, and we walked down the dark hall and into her bedroom. She climbed into bed, and I pulled the covers up to her neck. I could see the dark form of her face in the gloom.

"You're fine now," I said, and I began to walk out the door.

"Justin?" she peeped.

I stopped and turned. "What?" I asked.

"I'm thirsty," she said.

Oh, for crying out loud, I thought.

I walked down the hall, turned the corner, and went into the kitchen. The kitchen was dark, but a clock on the stove gave enough light to see.

I pulled out a plastic cup from the cupboard and filled it almost to the top, then I walked back to Maria's bedroom.

"Here's your—"

I stopped speaking.

Maria wasn't in her bed. She was standing by her window, looking out into the fog.

"*I told you,*" she whispered, her face pressed against the glass. "*I told you there was something in*

204

the fog."

And when I saw what it was, I gasped. I dropped the cup and it tumbled to the floor, spilling water all over the carpet and my feet.

But I didn't notice it. I just kept staring, horrified at what was in the fog beyond the bedroom window.

There was something in the fog.

I could see it.

I could *feel* it.

The murky, white mist drifted like a dream beneath the streetlight.

But that wasn't the problem.

The problem was the large, blurry shape that was standing by the side of the road.

It was hard to see. The fog was so thick that I could only make out the fuzzy shape of —

Something.

What was it?

"I told you so," Maria said in a sing-song

voice. She never moved, and we both kept staring at the form in the fog.

"What . . . what is it?" I managed to stammer.

Maria shook her head slowly.

"I don't know," she replied. "But I'm afraid. I don't like it."

I was afraid too, but I didn't tell Maria. I guess I didn't want her to know that I was terrified, just like she was. That would make her even *more* afraid.

I tip-toed slowly across the floor and stood next to her. My warm breath caused the glass to steam up, and I leaned back a little to keep from breathing on the window.

All the while, the strange form in the mist remained frozen, like it was staring back at us.

It was big, too. I couldn't tell for sure just how big it was, because the fog was too thick.

And then . . . *it moved.*

Maria gasped, and drew away from the window. She grasped my arm with both hands and held on tight.

"Justin . . . Justin . . . I'm scared. I'm really, really scared."

"It's . . . it's okay," I told her. I hoped that she couldn't sense the fear in my voice. "I'm . . . I'm sure that it's nothing. It's—"

The large form in the fog suddenly slunk into the shadows and disappeared.

Whatever it was, we couldn't see it anymore. It had vanished in the shadows of the unknown, where darkness slept and the beasts of the night dwelled.

And I was relieved. I didn't know what we had seen, and something told me that I didn't want to know.

Maria was still gripping my arm tightly, and we continued staring out into the fog for a long time.

Nothing.

No creature, no shape, no misty form.

Maria let go of my arm and climbed back into bed.

"I'm still afraid," she squeaked.

"It's gone," I told her. "Besides . . . whatever it was, it's outside. It can't get in our house."

I was wrong, of course, as I would soon find out.

I said good-night to Maria, walked to her bedroom door, and took one more quick glance out her window.

Just in case.

Just in case the form in the fog had returned.

I searched the murky mist beneath the streetlight, but I didn't see anything.

"Thanks Justin," Maria squeaked sleepily.

I left her door open, and walked silently down the dark hall and into my bedroom.

Outside my window, the fog seemed to have gotten even thicker. I had never, ever, seen fog so thick. I've heard the expression of fog being so thick that you could cut it with a knife.

That's just what it looked like. I was certain that if I went outside with my pocketknife, I would be able to cut a square from the fog and bring it back inside.

I strode over to my window to close the drapes. I'm not saying that I was chicken or anything, but the fog was really freaking me out.

And what about that . . . that *thing* Maria and I had seen? What was it?

Was it still out there? Out there in the fog?

I stared out the window, gazing into the hazy white.

And something moved.

In the shadows.

Near the bushes by our porch. Something moved. It ducked into the shadows, like it was trying to hide from me.

My blood ran cold. My heart started hammering again, like it had when Maria had come to my bedroom door.

What was it?

What was creeping around at night, slipping through the fog like a cat?

My breath had steamed up the window again, and I took a step back. The steam on the window faded away.

And I watched.

I looked into the shadows of the bushes. I strained my eyes to see deeper into the fog.

The creature had vanished again.

Just like before. When we were in Maria's room.

"I'm just glad I'm inside," I whispered to myself. *"I'm glad I'm inside where it can't get me."*

Whatever it is.

I breathed a sigh of relief. I was tired, and I was about to turn and climb back into my cozy bed.

It was then that I felt the icy fingers, bony and cold, wrap tightly around my neck.

VISIT:
WWW.AMERICANCHILLERS.COM

to find out more about this exciting NEW book series from Johnathan Rand! Read sample stories for FREE, and join the official American Chillers Fan Club! Plus, check out Mr. Rand's on-line journal, featuring pictures and stories during his journeys! It's like traveling with him yourself! You'll get the inside scoop on when and where he'll be, and what projects he's working on right now!

ABOUT THE AUTHOR

Johnathan Rand is the author of more than 65 books, with well over 4 million copies in print. Series include **AMERICAN CHILLERS, MICHIGAN CHILLERS, FREDDIE FERNORTNER, FEARLESS FIRST GRADER**, and **THE ADVENTURE CLUB.** He's also co-authored a novel for teens (with Christopher Knight) entitled **PANDEMIA.** When not traveling, Rand lives in northern Michigan with his wife and three dogs. He is also the only author in the world to have a store that sells only his works: **CHILLERMANIA!** is located in Indian River, Michigan. Johnathan Rand is not always at the store, but he has been known to drop by frequently. Find out more at:

www.americanchillers.com

FUN FACTS ABOUT OHIO:

State Capitol: Columbus

Became a state in 1803

17th state in the Union

State Bird: Cardinal

State Reptile: Black Racer

State Animal: White-Tailed Deer

State Tree: Buckeye

State Rock Song: *Hang On Sloopy*
by the McCoys

State Flower: Red Carnation

State Beverage: Tomato Juice

The state of Ohio encompasses 41,330 square miles

SOME FAMOUS PEOPLE FROM OHIO

☞ **Thomas Edison,** inventor of the incandescent light bulb and the phonograph is from Milan, Ohio

☞ The **Wright Brothers, Orville** and **Wilbur**, the first to fly an airplane, owned a bicycle shop in Dayton, Ohio

☞ **Garrett Morgan**, inventor of the first traffic light, hails from Cleveland

☞ **James Ritty,** the inventor of the cash register in 1878, was from Dayton

☞ **John Lambert,** maker of America's first automobile in 1891, was from Ohio City

☞ **Charles Goodyear** invented the process of vulcanizing rubber in 1839. Goodyear was from Akron.

*Other famous people from Ohio include track star **Jesse Owens**, writer **Toni Morrison**, film maker **Stephen Spielberg**, astronauts **Neil Armstrong and John Glenn**, comedians **Bobe Hope and Phyllis Diller**, opera singer **Kathleen Battle**, sharpshooter **Annie Oakley**, and actors **Luke Perry, Drew Carey, Halle Berry, Paul Newman, Debra Winger, Doris, Day, Clark Gable, and Hal Holbrook**, among many others!*

Johnathan Rand travels internationally for school visits and book signings! For booking information, call:

1 (231) 238-0338!

www.americanchillers.com

ATTENTION YOUNG AUTHORS!
DON'T MISS

JOHNATHAN RAND'S

AUTHOR QUEST

THE DEFINITIVE WRITER'S CAMP
FOR SERIOUS YOUNG WRITERS

If you want to sharpen your writing skills, become a better writer, and have a blast, Johnathan Rand's Author Quest is for you!

Designed exclusively for young writers, Author Quest is 4 days/3 nights of writing courses, instruction, and classes at Camp Ocqueoc, nestled in the secluded wilds of northern lower Michigan. Oh, there are lots of other fun indoor and outdoor activities, too . . . but the main focus of Author Quest is about becoming an even better writer! Instructors include published authors and (of course!) Johnathan Rand. No matter what kind of writing you enjoy: fiction, non-fiction, fantasy, thriller/horror, humor, mystery, history . . . this camp is designed for writers who have this in common: they LOVE to write, and they want to improve their skills!

For complete details and an application, visit:

www.americanchillers.com

Join the official

AMERICAN CHILLERS

FAN CLUB!

**Visit
www.americanchillers.com
for details!**

www.americanchillers.com

#1: THE MICHIGAN MEGA-MONSTERS

When Rick Owens arrives at Camp Willow, he's ready for a week of fun. He's met two new friends: Sandy Johnson and Leah Warner, and the three are ready for an exciting week.

But when Rick spots strange tracks around his cabin, the campers realize that they aren't the only ones at the small, lakeside summer camp. And what about the legends that speak of giant, terrifying creatures that roam the swamp at night?

Soon, Rick, Sandy, and Leah find out that the legends of the Michigan Mega-Monsters aren't legends at all! The problem is: have they found out too late?

READ AMERICAN CHILLERS #1: The Michigan Mega-Monsters, available at bookstores everywhere, or order from the official on-line superstore at

www.americanchillers.com

All AudioCraft books are proudly printed, bound, and manufactured in the United States of America, utilizing American resources, labor, and materials.

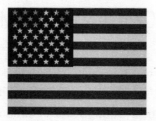

USA